Eyes U

Chatiela Underwood

Eyes Wide Shut

Chatiela Underwood

Published by
31 Woman LLC
7915 S. Emerson Ave Suite B-140
Indianapolis, Indiana 46237
www.31WomanLLC.com
info@31Woman.com
317-643-0769

LIBRARY OF CONGRESS: 2015936316

ISBN 10: 0983553491

ISBN 13: 978-0-9835534-9-6

Cover designed by: AMB Branding Design

Editing by Marcia Irvin and Chatiela Underwood

Printed in the United States of America

Dedication

I want to dedicate this book to the Lord and Savior Jesus Christ. My memories are attributed to Cory, baby we will forever miss and love you! To our prince, Aquileyce we made it through it together, mommy loves you babe! To my princess Cha'Nyveiah, you are my bundle of joy! You both are my blessings that I will forever be indebted to. Mommy loves the both of you to life and beyond!

To all my single mothers and fathers that have walked through the struggle doing what it takes to make it happen and make ends meet. To all the married couples that are going through it and hanging on by a thread but determined to make it happen. For all the soldiers that have been deployed and sacrificed their lives and families I salute you with love, peace, and prosperity! "Thank you for serving our country." To my college students struggling to make it happen, just roll up your sleeves and do it. It will be well worth it in the end. If anybody can do it, you can! To our homosexual community, those suffering with mental disorders, been rapped, or in abusive relationships. This is for you! I know we have common goals of pushing to continue overcoming challenges of adversity on the daily bases. If you're trying to break down those barriers to make it happen, my advice to you is to just keep on pushing on!

-Thank You!-

Acknowledgements

Wow, where do I began? I have to first Thank the man above. Thank you for all of the blessings that you have bestowed upon me and for the ones that are on their way! Without you I wouldn't of had the breathe in me to share my story! Mom you are my right hand and you have given me back bone to set out and reach my goals. You have showed me how to become a strong women. I love you Mom and dad!

To my family I appreciate you, and love you to pieces. Thank you Aunt Mi-Mi for being my confidant, and inspiring me to fulfill my dreams and to always finish what I start. Melvin, Andrea, and Joshua Thank you little brothers for keeping me grounded and blessing me with all of my beautiful nieces and nephews.

To My Publisher/Cousin, Charlotte of 31WOMEN LLC., thank you so much for all your relentless support, wisdom, determination and persistence to guide me through this journey! I appreciate and Love you so much for your patience!

To all my friends who either helped, encouraged, or motivated me and touch my life in any way Thank you so much! Shawna, Summer, David, Marcia, Jordan, Marva, Tryyun, Marsha, Erica, Jordan,, Rubina, America Maraj, Stephanie, Alicia and Ronnike for motivating me during this challenging process. Living it was one thing but putting the pen to paper was another. This was such a humbling experience and one that I wouldn't change for the world.

I can't not mention my best friend Kevin, and my spiritual family for your support, patience, and encouragement . Thank you so much, I love you for that! Friends and family if I did not mention you, Please forgive me in advance and know that I love you too!

~Many Blessings to you Always,~

Contents

Chapter 1

I had just gotten off work when my phone rang. Not noticing the number I muted it as I was way too tired to talk to anyone. Shortly after, I pulled up to mommies' house. Suddenly, a strong since of grief consumed me. It was such an over whelming, unsettling weird feeling like never before. Honestly it felt as if I was losing something. I hadn't had that feeling before, so I was filling a little uneasy, more like on edge! Let's just say I was feeling some type of way, with anxiety as it was the unknown factor that consumed me. When I stepped inside her house I immediately headed towards the bedroom to check on her.

"Mommy are you okay?" I asked.

"Yeah baby why you ask"? She replied!

My phone rang again this time it was my house number that showed across the caller ID. "What now!" I thought to myself? "Hello."

"Sis, Where you at?" My baby brother, Samuel asked.

"Over moms house why?"

"Carter just called and said something is wrong." Sam told me in a panicked voice! "Something is real wrong."

"What do you mean, what happed" I asked him.

"He called and asked where you were? I told him you were at work! He then asked to speak with Armando. I told him he was asleep and he told me to wake him up because this may be the last time he talk to him."

"What do you mean the last time?" I asked.

"I don't know sis, all he said was something about the police is at his house and that I need to wake Armando up. By the time I got back to the phone he had hung up. I tried to call him back but he didn't answer.

I'm scared sis, he didn't seem or sound like himself." My brother sounded frantic, which sent my mind racing one-hundred miles per millisecond. "Something's up, sis, something's not right! You have to find out what the hell is going on and then call me right back!"

The phone call with my brother left my mind racing; which had bad thoughts flooding my mind. My phone then rang again; it was that strange number from before. "Who could this be?" I thought to myself I don't normally answer numbers that I don't know but something told me I should answer this one. "Hello" I answered.

It was Carter on the other end, He was in a rage, his voice was deep and monotone as if he had been drinking and taking his medication at the same time. He definitely didn't sound like his normal self. He was screaming at me from the top of his lungs. All I could make out of what he was saying is BITCH as the phone was going in and out sounding warped.

There was a beating noise in the background and it sounded like it was the door. "Bam, bam, bam. I heard it again. Who the hell is that and what's going on?" I asked.

"Carter, open the door. Come out!" the voice on the other end said.

"What in the world is going on" I yelled? "Who is that Carter?"

"We have you surrounded just come out now and surrender." The voice yelled in the background. "We have the premises secure! You need to come out with your hands up!"

"The police at the door and I told them cats I ant coming out! Between you, Monique and that wife of mine you bitches have pushed me over the edge! Take care of my son! Do you hear me? Take care of my damn son. I was in total shock. "Do you hear me storm?"

Mommy heard me talking and grabbed the phone from me. "Carter, what's going on baby? She asked him with her concerned motherly voice.

"Oh, Ms. Darlene! I'm sorry, I didn't know that was you I thought you were your daughter!"

"Baby, what's wrong with you?"

"I can't do this shit no more, and I want you and Storm to take care of my boy! I don't know if I'm going to make it out of here but I want her to take care of my baby boy!" He said in a pleading but demanding voice.

The call dropped and all I heard was the dial tone! I was confused, scared, concerned, and that made me panic. The thought of what the hell was about to happen sent chills through my body, and shook my core like no other. A sense of fear accompanied me, I couldn't shake it. For some reason it felt like that was going to be our last conversation. Right then, the TV show was interrupted with breaking news;

"Just in a military man holding himself hostage in his apartment. Swat team is clearing out the block for a possible standoff near the Air Force Base.

"What the hell!" I thought to myself. I didn't have time to stand there and process what he just said or what the news was talking about. I had to get there and fast! I knew there was no good to come of this! I had to get there to save him from whatever it was he had going on!

Sitting there thinking about it wasn't going to get me any answers. I picked up our son and went flying on route 4, the highway connector. All I was wondering was what was the bottom line? What was the reason behind him snapping, this time? I wanted to be well informed, so

I could approach him one on one, and calm him down! I didn't see red lights, stop signs or anything. All I could do is drive.

I pulled up speeding as if I was still on the highway. I turned right on to the corner of where his apartment sits and as soon as our baby boy seen it he got excited.

"Mommy, we're at my daddy's house!" He started yelling from the back seat, Dada house mommy. Yay, I get to see my Dada!"

I didn't know how to respond or know what to say. All I seen were flashing lights, news vans from every station, and reporters from everywhere. There were police from every district including, the military police, and not to mention the swat team. It seemed surreal as if I was playing a star role in a bad dream. I was confused as to why law enforcement and reporters where here and just for Carter.

This was more like a nightmare that I couldn't wake up from, although I kept pinching my face. Shit was real and unfortunately, my reality. I just can't believe this was really happening to us! Everything seemed like it was playing out in slow motion and all our plans and dreams were going down the drain.

I jumped out the car to get the baby out his car seat.

"Ma'am, Ma'am, who are you?" a reporter asked but I ignored her. I ignored them as long as I could. A bunch of reporters ran my way catching me off guard. They put the cameras straight on us.

"Ma'am, who are you?" the same reporter asked, which irritated the hell out of me.

Lights were shining bright directly in our faces. The glare was blinding us. My son started crying and gripped me tighter. Tighter than ever before and it scared me shitless. "Momma is Dada ok?" My baby asked me with tears rolling down his face.

"Ma'am how do you know the person inside?" one of the reporters asked. "

"My name is Storm, and this is our son. Carter is his father and I need to get in there so he can see his son?" I told her.

The women reporter to the left of me came and got directly in my face.

"Can I ask you a few questions?" As she pulled out her micro phone. Giving me no time to answer or rebuttal. She told me to state my name and the relation you are to the man inside. Then she asked if there was one thing that I could say to him right now what would it be? I turned to the camera and said don't make any rational decisions babe, please come out we need you! At that moment, Armando cried for his Dada. I guess he was starting to figure out something was wrong. After those words, I immediately headed towards Carter's apartment, holding my son tighter than ever. There was a truck full of SWAT. The negotiator headed my direction. Once he locked eyes with me, he signaled for me.

I wanted to act like I didn't see him, but I was too afraid of that big ass gun so, I went anyway.

"Ma'am how do you know the subject?"

"Excuse me," I replied.

"How do you know him? He asked?

I further explained to him that this was my ex, my son's father. "He called me saying some crazy shit so, I need to get in there sir please." I pleaded with the officer.

"Did you just tell me that he called you?"

He asked with his eyebrows raised.

"Yes sir!" I replied.

The negotiator told me, "They had been trying to get ahold of Carter since earlier this evening, when he called 911 and were unsuccessful. He told me that Carter called 911 and said that he was thinking about killing himself.

"What?" I screamed.

"What did he say to you?" He asked.

After rambling off the story again. He asked me, "Is he a threat to us, ma'am?"

" I looked at him with a blank face, hesitant. Not wanting to answer.

"Ma'am, is he a threat to us?" As if I didn't hear him the first time. "Is he a threat to himself?" The officer asked. I told him that, he had done this stunt a few other times. This doesn't surprise me.

"We know and we are very well acquainted. He informed me. "We've had a run in with him before at a club.

"That's news to me." I told him. The officer ended up telling me that apparently Carter had the club shut down because of his thoughtless actions that particular night.

Oh yea, Carter knows us very well." The negotiator commented.

"When? Are you kidding me?" I was in total shock. I never knew that he did something of this magnitude in public.

That was the first I heard of that shenanigans and you think you know someone after eight years!

"What number did he call you from because the number we have is disconnected? I hesitated, but it was too late. Besides, I had already told him that he called me so I couldn't back paddle now. I walked straight into that one and there was no exit, or fixing it at this point. Damn I thought to myself! Damn it, Damn it, Damn it I yelled as I looked through my phone slowly, just trying to stall time a little more and think of a way to get out of it. I couldn't think of one fast enough so I gave him the correct number. "Ma'am I need you to stay put" He told me as he walked away towards the others.

A few minutes later he returned. "Ma'am we have been unsuccessful with contacting him. He has ceased all communication with us. We are going to disconnect his phone, turn off his power and water." He nonchalantly explained to me.

"Excuse me" I yelled. What the fuck do you mean? You can't do that." I said in a panic.

"Well ma'am, he is refusing all communication with us. I have no other choice. We can't even get him on the phone to talk to us at this point." He logically explained. "We have cleared out the block and I'm going to need you and your son to go over there in the secure, safe area." He pointed signaling me to go across the street he said, we're going in!"

My heart sank. "Sir please, you cannot do that to him!" I cried, screamed and pleaded. "He just returned from war! He has mental issues because of it! You can't just cut his utilities off like that sir. He's going to feel like his back is against the wall likes he's back in Iraq. You'll leave him with no other choice but to go into war mode." I explained "He is bipolar and schizophrenic. Don't do that sir please." I powerlessly cried.

"Ma'am, we need you and your son to step over there. This area is dangerous. Bullets may start flying so

I need you to go immediately!" He yelled ignoring my concerns. I pleaded with him falling to the ground, praying for a miracle. I felt hopeless and helpless as I knew that was my last chance at saving him.

"Ma'am get up!" He demanded with a stern voice "You have to go now!"

I continued pleading with him, screaming, begging. I was trying as a last attempt to convenience him to change his mind and try another tactic.

"Sir, all he needs to do is see his son. Can you just let us in so I can talk to him and can convince him to come out without force?" I yelled. "I know this man! I know what I'm doing. Just let me try please! I can get through to him and make this end peacefully. I don't want his life in jeopardy.

"Ma'am, we cannot do that because you never know a person mental state. We deal with this all the time. We can't be held responsible if he kills you and your son." I through myself to him with tears falling like a waterfall.

"Please listen to me, he would never hurt me or his son. He has tried to kill himself two times before and I've been successful at talking him out of it. He needs me. I know what I'm doing I know this man. He just needs to be reassured that everything is ok."

"Here's what we need to do, I'll keep our son out here with you, and just let me go in for, Christ sake Dam! Sir please" I cried.

Still ignoring my cries, he turned his back away from me and signaled at the others, with his hand. They began marching towards the apartment in unison. I couldn't believe what I was witnessing. I felt my heart skip beats. I think I stopped breathing. This felt like a bad dream gone wrong, and I couldn't wake up from it. There were a squad of swat. The first one had a shield and something that looked like a machine gun. The others had their guns drawn moving in on him marching closer. That scared the hell out me. They had snipers on the roofs, which I felt was very unnecessary.

The negotiator said they had to treat him like that because he was military and trained like one of them. I screamed and cried helplessly. I kept calling his phone, hung up and called again at least a hundred times. I'd never ask for a miracle or prayer until this moment in my life. All I wanted to do was hear his voice more than anything in this world.

Armando was so afraid and confused because he didn't know what was going on. I was pissed. There was nothing that I could have done and it was out of my control. I didn't know what else to do I just wanted to let him know they were coming in. Our son just kept screaming. I had to get him out of there and alive. I tried to call his phone again, this time it went straight to voicemail. Damn they cut the mutha fucka off!

GROWING PAINS

Let's start from the beginning. Nine Years Earlier....

All I wanted to do is lie in the bed with the blinds closed, pillow over my head, basically hiding from the outside world. I felt like a hopeless romantic, scared of the unknown, mad at the fact that I'd given four years to James and he had been living a double life. James was a guy that I was in a relationship with right before my son's father. He was one way with me and obviously another when he was being his true self.

My girlfriends kept calling. All day my phone rang. I'd look at it only to put it on silent. The thought of what I had just found out was embarrassing, overwhelming and it made me feel nauseous. My stomach cringed every time I envisioned the fact of reality in my head.

Wow, was all I could say in disbelief. I broke down in tears just thinking about it. Soon after the phone calls stopped my doorbell rang.

"Who the hell is it"? I yelled as I walked towards the door.

I couldn't tell you the last time I had showered, combed my hair, or even went outside. That is why I was reluctant to answer. All I wanted to do was be alone and host my own pity party. I tried to stand up but I didn't have the energy. I felt weak as if I was going to faint. I looked out the peep hole and wasn't surprised to see who it was on the other side of the door.

I decided to open it, and was immediately blinded by the sun. My best friend was standing there looking like she was ready to kick in the door had I not answered.

"Girl, you are going to make me kick my foot up your behind! What's wrong with you? I'm worried about you!" she told me going on and on. "Why haven't you

23

been answering my calls? You should have known I was coming over to check on you!"

There was one question after another, and I didn't get a chance to answer any of them! I looked at her with the meanest look and replied I didn't feel like being bothered.

Of course she wasn't having that.

"You need to get out this dam house and back on the scene. You're a single black female now and you can't let him being gay take you out the game like this, boo. You had no control over what he decided to do with his life." She explained. "All you can do is pick up and move on. Look at yourself, I've never seen you like this!"

Hearing those words coming out of her mouth was reality all over again. It was like a knife stabbing me in my heart, or more like pouring salt on an open wound. Tears started falling from my face faster than a water faucet.

I headed for the bedroom, I needed to lie back down. She followed behind me.

"So, what's going on with James? Have you'll talked yet and does he know that you know?" she asked.

"No, we haven't talked and he doesn't have a clue that I know." I told her.

Shaking her head in disbelief she said, "I can't believe that he would deceive you this way." Jade responded, "Girl I'm not trying to be insensitive but I told you something wasn't right with him.

I think I need to take some time off from relationships and focus more in myself and my studies. Hell a man is the last thing that I need right now" I further explained to Jade.

"I'm so sorry you had to go through this storm. I wouldn't wish this on my worst enemy." She told me, "The most important thing is that you get checked out first thing. You need to make an appointment at the clinic because there is no telling who he done slept with. In the mean time you need to get yourself together. Let's go dancing she said. Like old times. I'm getting your butt out of this house tonight, and I'm not taking no for an answer! So, get up and get ready. I'll be back to pick you up in few" she said.

I have no understanding! I knew our relationship seemed strained lately, but I never thought it would end up like this. First, he started canceling our dates. Then, he, to my surprise, started cancelling me. And that was unlike him as we were inseparable.

His odd behavior was a red flag and made me suspicious. My womanly instincts and inspector gadget kicked in and told me to check his messages. He gave me his password a few months back. I'd never used it before but he gave it to me to use not stare at it. So I decided to use it. I had been staring at the code for a while, however, I finally gained up the courage to check it. Sadly, I trusted him and thought that this may just be a waste of time checking, but the voice in the back of my mind had me afraid because I didn't know what I was about to find out!

I couldn't believe what I was hearing. My mouth dropped and arms went numb. All I could do was sit in a bottle of confusion. I couldn't help but start pressing number one to listen to the next message, and the next. And why did I do that?

I opened up a can of worms and a door I couldn't shut back. I was glad that I went with my gut feelings to listen to his voicemails but I was more so in shock from what I was hearing. I couldn't believe it. There were a few more voicemails that I screened through and I couldn't help but notice the men trying hard to sound like women, and referring to my man as Peaches! Who the hell was Peaches I thought to myself? I instantly grew disgusted!

I dropped the phone, and started screaming. I went and stood in the shower for hours it seemed like, with my clothes on. I haven't answered any of his calls and he didn't have the slightest clue that I knew.

Supposedly, he was flying out to Chicago and L.A. next week to do drag queen shows. The men on his voicemail were all looking to set up dates and hook up's during his visit at the club. I wonder how long this been going on? And how long he has been putting my life in jeopardy. Sadly, I trusted him.

The thought of my man sleeping with other men was nasty, dangerous, unacceptable and more so, something I couldn't compete with. My man was gay; doing drag shows, hanging out in gay clubs, competing in beauty pageants. The only diva around here is me, and no room for two of us. I instantly felt sick and scared. The scariest part was the unknown. Did he give me something? Was he sick? Oh My God!

I didn't have a clue that he was interested in men, or how long he had been doing it. I don't even know if he has AIDs for that matter. I kept asking myself why I didn't get the memo of him being on the down low.

This is something I defiantly didn't see coming. Nor did I have a clue that men was where his interest lied. He was an undercover brother, and that is not cool to me. I judge no one but if you are going to have sex with both genders I think you should keep your partners informed. Give them a chance to make an informed decision, use protection, and allow them respect and options. Hell life is too short I thought to myself and I have a purpose on this earth to live!

I couldn't help but reminisce back to all the times we were out in public and people would look at us and start whispering or laughing. You know how side bar conversations go. It was quite obvious that we were being talked about and laughed at. I hadn't a clue for what they were laughing at. That is until now! When we were out together one particular day, a woman even ask if we were brother and sister. After replying no. She asked me if I were dumb or blind and casually walked away giving me no chance to respond.

I always thought that he just had mannerism because he was raised the old school way by his grandparents. James had a certain swag about him in the beginning but I guess you can't judge a book by its cover. He wore suits every day and I can't even lie that's what attracted me to him. He wasn't an average guy by any means. I was young and more so naïve'.

I didn't really know what I wanted in a man, hell, I was still trying to find myself. With an absent father, as a female, I really didn't know how to interact in a relationship. I didn't have a male role model and lacked the tour guide of a father to show me. I couldn't tell you exactly what I wanted in a man back then but I can tell you at this moment what I don't want! I knew that eventually James and I would talk, and I had to mentally prepare myself for this as I wasn't looking forward to it. Honesty, I wanted to avoid him as long as I could, and he was the last person I wanted to see.

In the meantime, I really needed to get out of this house so I decided to take Jade up on her offer and go out with the ladies. It was long overdue and much needed, so I agreed. I definitely wasn't going to find a peace of mind in the house, I thought to myself! Hell, I had nothing to lose nor did I have anything better to do for the evening. Lying around moping, crying all day, was getting old. So, I decided to go with my girls and change up my environment!

I made a cocktail, and blared my Jill Scott music. I was determined to let my hair down and go out. All I wanted to do is have a good time it was well overdue. I had to shake myself out of this funk like Jade advised. After all, she was right.

I'm young, sexy, educated and have a lot to offer the right man! I can't roll over and play dead now. I have to jump back on the scene because I have a whole life ahead of me. So, I called my girl to let her know that I was taking her up on her offer.

"Great, then I'm going to get dressed and I'll be there in a few to pick you up."

"Alright girl, I'll be ready." I replied. I took a long hot shower for what felt like hours and smoked one. I wanted to reflect on what the hell I was going through and come up with a plan of action to get my mind back right.

I looked over myself in the mirror. My makeup was flawless, and my lace front looked like I was fresh out the shop. I wore a black mini dress that hugged every curve in all the right places. My all black ambiance couldn't be pulled off without something to make it pop like the matching red four inch stilettos and accessories. I was starting to feel a little better about myself. I felt that I really needed this. As good as I was looking, I have to admit my swag would be a little extra tonight!

Hotspot nightclub was where all the military and college students hung out. Going out really wasn't my thing and I knew I had finals next week. I felt like I owed it to myself to let my hair down so to speak, let loose and enjoy myself with the girls. Have a good time for a change, I needed to get my mind off things and escape the reality of what was going on in my life.

About nine thirty that evening, I heard the horn so I took one last look in the mirror. I shed a happy tear. I was proud of myself because I looked so drastically different from the person I was a few hours earlier. I grabbed my keys, purse and dashed for the door.

"Dam! Girl, look at you!

Now that's the Storm I know. You've just done a total transformation. A few hours ago you looked like shit." Jade said in a jokingly way. "I'm just kidding" she said with a fake chuckle.

"I'm so happy you came out with us boo. You had me scared there for a minute. You haven't been answering my calls and avoiding us." Gina said, co-signing in the back seat. "Please don't do that again or we are going to have some serious problems baby girl!

Gina, Jade and I grew up together. Jade is a smart, cute, petite woman and more on the reserve side. She's known for her brick house body and being about her business. She went to Wilberforce which is the other HBCU across the street from my school, Central State University so we were inseparable.

As soon as we walked in the club I couldn't help but notice the mirrors alongside the dance floor. The music was blaring and the dance floor was packed from wall to wall. That was my cue. There were military guys everywhere. It was college night so there were a lot of students and alumni from my school and other local colleges. All of the Greeks from the Devine Nine was stepping but all I seen where the sophisticated pink and green girls better known as Alpha Kappa Alpha Sorority Incorporated and the red and white Delta diva's. So, you already know it was most definitely the place to be tonight!

I took a deep breath and examined my surroundings. I couldn't help but notice the cutie eye balling me from across the room on the dance floor. This brother caught my eye at first glance. I started dancing and moving towards him. He started grinning from ear to ear and started towards my way. All I saw were pearly white teeth but at least that was confirmation that he weren't missing any.

He finally started walking towards my way. "Hi beautiful, my name is Carter." He introduced himself in a sexy tone. "Are you here alone or with your man?" he asked.

He was so fine I almost couldn't respond. "My name is Storm. I'm here with my girls and no I don't have a man." I told him.

Once we introduced ourselves to one another we ended up talking, dancing and laughing the whole night standing in the same spot. Both of our friends kept coming over giving signals and hints trying to get us to come leave but they were unsuccessful. They must've started wondering if we forgot who we came to the club with because we didn't see them again until we were on our way out of the club a few hours later.

The next morning I recall it was about nine a.m. When Carter called and invited me to breakfast and a party on the Air force base. He told me to pack a bag of some gym clothes so we can stop by the gym.

"The gym, wait a minute Carter! I don't know you like that! He interrupted and said "But you're going to get to know me!"

I like his confidence. "Well I guess I could go with you under one circumstance", I told him.

"What's that?" he asked.

"You have to show my brother your license when you get here." I told him.

He chuckled and said "That's no problem babe. I got you, I will be there in thirty minutes! Do you need me to bring you anything?" he asked.

"No, thank you! I replied, I was caught off guard. He seemed to be such a gentlemen and I can respect a man with such stature. "Where do you live at anyway?"

"I live on base in the housing dorms. I got a suite mate but he's a cool guy."

What the hell, I thought to myself, I was game!

I was nervous and very excited that he had called so soon. I like the spontaneity, it was a turn on. I had never dated or been interested in a military man before, so I was definitely excited. I liked what I saw more than anything. He was definitely not hard on the eyes, at least from what I could remember, I'll be the first to admit, I had one too many cocktails at the club the night I met him.

I do recall he was polished, muscular built, Bo legged and sexy with a mouthpiece. He seemed a little more mature and much different from what I was used to.

Carter was a laid back, outgoing, funny, lovable, adventurous and a very responsible type of guy. I turned into someone different overnight. Just yesterday, I was consumed with life changing news about James. However, today I was on to the next, better and real man! Wow, the man upstairs work in mysterious ways. My life changed right before me, James being gay was the furthest thing on my mind right now.

I wanted to freshen up before he came through. I wasn't sure what to wear but I wanted to look good for him. After looking and changing outfits for what seemed like forever, I finally decided to go with a brown dress with a red and brown floral print scarf for my neck and all the accessories to match. I was hoping that I wasn't overdressed, as usual. But it would be unlike me if I wasn't. My Mac makeup was flawless and my hair was a breeze when I threw on my lace front. So it looked like I had just left the beauty shop.

I panicked when he told me to bring gym shoes. I chuckled didn't know how to tell him I didn't own any. I only owned a lot of heels. Diva status over here, stilettos only!

About a half hour later he pulled up in an old school, blue Cadillac with nice shinny rims in the snow. I was always taught to never drive your expensive rims through the snow. But, to each his own. I looked out the window and watched him struggling up to the house. We had every bit of five feet of snow. Once he got in the house his eyes grew big as he looked down at my feet.

"You don't have any gym shoes?"

I told him no, I don't own any.

"Well I'm going to have to change that." He said with a mischievous smile.

It has been two weeks now since I met Carter and I have not been back home since. We had so much in common we became inseparable. We've been locked in his dorm room. A one room box with a bed, dresser, mini refrigerator, TV, and pictures of his family all over the walls strung with Christmas lights and it wasn't even Christmas. The lights looked as if they been up for a couple of years with all the dust they have collected.

Attached to the room was a bathroom that he shared with his suite mate, Iman. So two people shared a bathroom. Iman was very interesting to meet to say the least. He was from Iraq, studying in school to be a doctor. He was already a labor and delivery nurse for the U.S. Air force. His family was still overseas and his father was a figure on a video game. I'd never met anyone like him although I met a lot of unique people from all over the country. I can say, military people know how to party.

I was excited and fascinated with the new scenery. I had never been on a military base let alone lived, shopped and partied there. I saw every inch of the base when we came up for air. Sometimes, we'd miss lunch at the chow hall so we would walk ten steps to the right to burger king. It wasn't something that I'd normally eat but what could I say we were both being lazy.

The chow hall was amazing to see for the first time. There were different lines for various selections of food. They had a variety, something like a buffet restaurant. You could sit and watch TV on one of the many flat screens on the walls while eating your food. As I looked around, I seen so much diversity. People from all walks of life sitting and enjoying lunch and dinner in uniform with co-workers and family. I couldn't help but notice how happy everyone appeared. There sat rows of tables and booths along the wall for sitting space. It seemed to have a lot of traffic come through but never filled to capacity. When the uniformed men and women came in I noticed that they all took their hats off at the door. I didn't see a single person wearing one.

Carter spoiled me rotten. I could get use to this I silently thought to myself. So far, he has been nothing but a perfect gentleman, and the first real man I've been with. I was starting to fall for him and fast. I kind of think he was feeling the same way. He'd drop me off on the yard at CSU, when he went to work and picked me back up when he got off every day. He didn't miss a beat. I missed being in his presence each day as I watched him pull away. However, I was also happy that he was going to take care of business and I would soon be back in his arms. If this is how love feels I thought to myself then what I had with my James was lust.

Carter invited me this weekend to go with him to a party at the CO'S Club which is for the officers of the Air Force. It's where they host parties and had a bar set up, pool tables, TV, food, etc. It's very nice. He'd introduced me to a few of his female friends on base a few days prior. So, we were all to meet up there. I, of course wanted to dress to kill so I had him take me to the mall to get a dress for the evening.

Like I said before military people know how to party. By the time he introduced me to what seemed like the fiftieth person I was barely able to stand due to all the alcohol. I kept trying to tell him I was not a drinker. Every time I looked up he was handing me another cocktail. I told him I'd rather smoke but being that we were on base smoking was not allowed.

"Come on babe let's go" he said while grabbing my hand and waist. We headed towards the dorms walking in the dark. Be careful he said as I was staggering and stumbling with no contacts in. This was my first experience being drunk and I didn't know what to do. I went to take the next step and he yelled stop and grabbed me at the same time as tight as he could. I didn't realize I was about to step in a cemented open pit partially filled with water in the middle of the field. He saved my life!

"You're done" he said while picking me up and carrying me up the steps into his dorm room. He's strong as hell I thought to myself. I'd never had a man carry me like this either. He opened the door and put me in the bed. He then turned on a flick and went to the bathroom. Shortly after, I heard the shower turn on. I couldn't believe what I was looking at. Carter retuned butt naked dripping wet standing there bowlegged as hell with his sexy ass. The room was still spinning and it sounded like the moaning noise got louder from the porn on the television. When I went to jump out the bed my legs went limp as noodles and I threw up all over myself. Unable to get up I just laid there. He then took all my clothes off without hesitation and carried me to the shower and washed me up.

"Stay right here" he said as I leaned against the wall. He returned with his tee shirt and a pair of his shorts.

"Put this on" he said handing me something to relax in. I was embarrassed to say the least, so I locked the door and stayed in the restroom a long time. He and his suite mate knocked on the door at the same time wondering if I was ok.

"Here I come" I yelled.

"What's taking so long?" Carter asked with concern.

"Hey Iman", I said as I walked out of the restroom. I totally forgot that he shared a restroom with his roommate. I was so embarrassed but I kept my cool. When I went in the room my man had cleaned my mess up and made the bed without any complaints. I thanked him for doing that because I was on my way to attempt cleaning it up myself. I did not want to kiss him with my throw up breath even though I brushed my teeth, I was uncomfortable. That was sweet of him to do that because I didn't have the stomach for it I would of threw up again.

Everything seemed so right, we just clicked and bonded real fast, and grew inseparable. I was falling head over heels for him at this point. He was very responsible, well mannered, mature, handsome, outgoing, and knew how to treat a women. He made me feel special, you know like the way a grown women should feel!

"Baby I have to tell you something. These last couple of weeks have been great, and everything have been happening so fast. Listen, I care about you a lot Storm. I really do, your beautiful, intelligent, you are in school getting your degree and you're smart as hell. But I think we been moving a little too fast. My heart sank. He said we needed to slow down because he didn't want to get too attached."

"What do you mean you don't want to get attached?" I asked.

"I don't want to hurt you, Storm because I love you too much. I'll be leaving in a few weeks to go overseas."

"What are you talking about you don't want to hurt me? And you're leaving going where overseas?" I asked.

"I'm getting deployed."

"What does that mean?" I asked.

He further explained to me that he had to leave on military duty and may be gone for a half of year. I was speechless and didn't know what to say. I knew that I was with a military man, but the reality of what his job entailed just hit me. He was really leaving me going overseas to another country, and may be in harm's way. I realized how all of a sudden our daily routines would be coming to an end. Him, sleeping by my side every night would be no more, and we wouldn't be able to talk when we want. My life was about to change. The little things that I was use to I guess I took for granted. I never imagined that this day would ever come. I never realized the reality of his job until that moment.

Later that night I got a call from James, this was the first time that I heard from him since I found out he was on the down low. I can't say that I was ready to face him yet, I didn't have the words to describe how I felt. He had been missing in action and so had I. I had moved on and really didn't want to feel that pain and hurt again. Honestly, I tried to forget about him and didn't want to look back! Just remembering what he had done gave me the creeps all over again, so only the lord knows how this conversation was going to go. Against my better judgment I decided to finally talk to him. He talked and I listened, there was nothing he could possibly say to make me forgive him. He told me that he had been away getting his head together and had been going through a lot. At this point I'm uncertain about my future, and my health.

"What are you talking about?" I asked sounding annoyed.

"I've got something to tell you Storm, and I don't know how you're going to take this but just know that I love you. I never meant to hurt you, Storm. I've just been trying to find myself."

He paused for what seemed like two seconds and hesitantly said in a low voice "I like men. I've been secretly dating men behind your back."

I really didn't have the words to say, but before I could say anything his next words traumatized me, as it was the worst news and words you never want to hear. He said he recently got tested for HIV and found out that he was positive. He said since find out his life has changed so fast and that he had been accepted by the aids foundation. He said they were helping him with purchasing his medicine, housing, and giving him resources to dealing with it. I was lost of words and didn't know how to respond, or know what to say besides cursing him out and giving him the riot act. I mean what did he expect a pity party?

Storm, "You need to get tested!" He warned me. Bottom line storm I just wanted to let you know.

"Fine time to tell someone, don't you think?" I yelled.

"You should have told me you were interest in men before you touched me." "I mean you wasted my time, put my life in jeopardy, and literally tried to kill me with a virus."

"You don't care about me hell you never did or else you would have never did this to me. I don't think you even care about yourself I yelled."

"You better pray to god that you didn't infect me, or I'll take you out of here quicker than your disease!"

Storm, "I don't know if you have it or not but the best thing you can do is go get tested as well." he advised.

My mouth dropped, I was speechless, frustrated, sensed betrayal it felt like a dose of reality just hit me.

It felt like my life had flashed before my eyes and everything that I had worked so hard for was pointless. All I kept thinking is can you get AIDS with wearing condoms? Did he infect me? My mind was racing all I could think about is being exposed to an incurable disease. The thought of this was real scary. The next day I made an urgent appointment at the doctor's office, I needed to get tested. They managed to get me in the next day but said it would take one to two weeks for the results. I was very upset about that and sat on pins and needles and it felt like eternity. I also had to tell Carter the paralyzing news I'd just received. Hell we both needed to get tested, and I didn't know how he was going to take this.

Everything was happening so fast, all this news came at once and was a little too much to handle. I couldn't do anything but wonder how did this happened? How was I not able to see this coming? The last thing I wanted to do is give a false alarm so I had to wait for the test results. It seemed like the longest wait in my life.

Two grueling weeks later the results where forever life changing to me. All I could do is cry, jump up and down and be grateful to see I had a second chance at life. To know that I was that close to an infected man, and to see that my life was in jeopardy opened up my eyes. All I can say is the devil was busy and I knew the man upstairs had forever blessed me, God had my back! Fortunately, that chapter of my life was over, and I was ready to move forward with Carter knowing that I was disease free!

NORMAN

I stayed at my mother's house for the winter break. Her boyfriend and I did not get along at all. So, one day He decided to test me. I was lying in the living room watching TV, and Sonny came walking through the living room mumbling something under his breath.

"Excuse me," I asked him with attitude in my voice.

"You need to get a job and get the fuck out!" he demanded. I don't take disrespect lightly so I screamed as loud as I could so that he could hear me clear!

"You can't kick me out my momma house!" I told him.

All I know was that he came walking towards me cursing and then punched me in my jaw without hesitation. Caught me off guard! My instinct was to hold my jaw, but he kept coming at me, he picked me up and threw me. My mom came running from the bedroom.

"What's going on out here?" she yelled "Sonny stop" she said as he started punching me harder! "Stop Sonny now!" She jumped in the middle of us and looked him in his face. "You stop right now. You've gone too far! Now what happed?"

I jumped up and swung on him making contact with his chest. He then threw me through the glass decorated table that sat along the wall. When I realized my mom didn't have my back and sided with him, that was a pivotal moment in my life. Even though that hurt me to the core that was all the motivation I needed to stand on my own two feet and become a women. I knew that I could never live there ever again.

My mom told me that he didn't want me there.

"You two can't live under the same roof! This is breaking my heart but you're eighteen now. Here take this money" she told me as she pulled out one thousand dollars out of her purse.

"This should be enough for you to get an apartment. That's your first month rent and the deposit. You're on your own now baby girl."

Well what about the months after that the utilities and food every day? I don't even have a job yet ma." I cried.

"Honey you need to go get a job its time to stand on your own two feet. You can sleep on the couch for tonight but tomorrow you will have an apartment." Coincidently, that same night Carter ended up calling me from overseas. I didn't know where to start the fact that he beat me, or the part where they put me out and I don't have a place to live so I just started crying.

"What's wrong babe" he asked me.

"He hit me!"

"Who hit you?"

"Sonny did" I told him.

Not to mention we had already been talking about moving in together because the barracks was obvious not livable for the both of us and I was paying for my dorm room at Central that I was never in. By me not owning a vehicle, the commute back and forth from the base to school was killing Carter in gas.

I couldn't tell him the whole story before he cut me off. He said go to western union tomorrow and pick up some money find us a house before I get back from deployment.

"I'll send you a little extra so you can still go to the Kentucky Derby. Everything will work itself out babe cheer up.

My tears of anger and frustration became tears of joy because I realized that this man cared about me that much that he would go out of his way to take care of and protect me. The thought of him having my back made me feel more honored to be his woman.

"Thank you so much, Carter. You just do not know how much this means to me."

"Babe, it's going to be okay, I love you. And tell Sonny, I'll be to see him when I get back in the country. Keep your head up champ I should be home in about a month alright!"

He assured me "I love you I'll try to email you later."

"Okay be careful and I love you more." He hung up. Sad to say I never looked back on dysfunctional family.

It had been months now since he had been deployed and was due back home soon. I was starting to get bored and missing my man

This was the first time he had gone, so I had to find something to do with my time. Everyone seen a change in me lately and it seemed like everything was coming together for me despite everything. I kept myself busy, became more independent, and held down my new full time job while in school working towards my degree. I was proud of myself, Things were looking up I had my own money, car and still doing well in school. Now all I needed was a house and my man back safely.

It hadn't been to long since Carter returned home and he was still trying to get adjusted in the new house. Us living together fulltime, and being back from war. Life was coming at him fast. I quickly noticed that something was off and wrong.

Although we've known each other a few months before he deployed he seemed different from what I could remember.

The first thing he purchased when he came back home from overseas was three garden snakes, a rabbit, and pit bull names Showtime. If it wasn't an animal or reptile that he brought home it was a homeless person.

At this point he didn't discriminate everyone was his friend. I often joked and said he'd bring home a stray dog if I let him. Carter was having trouble sleeping, when he finally did he kept having bad nightmares about the war, and kept thinking people where after him. He was easily irritated and unexpectedly struggling trying to get adjusted and back to normal life again. I'd never seen anything like it. All I could suggest and ask is that he speaks to his superiors at work and go to the doctors because I didn't know how to help him.

He kept saying "it's okay." But clearly it wasn't.

In fact it was everything but.

His mother was due to be released from prison on an unknown case as he was reluctant to tell me.

All I knew is that he loved and missed her, and they often times wrote letters back and forth. He thought it would be a good time for him to reunite with her, as he had been very close with her over the years. His little brother Derrick grew up in foster care with various foster parents and we'd often get him from time to time. I thought bringing his family together would be healthy for his mental state right now. I loved this man so whatever it took I was willing to give it a try. At this point I was all in.

I didn't know what to expect but the visit went well. Carter and his brother had time to bond, and his mother and I had a chance to get to know each other. She was a very pretty lady but being from Nebraska I had to get her hair together if that was the last thing I done. After I took her to the casino, we stopped by the beauty salon so my friend could do her hair, and nails before leaving. We hit it off so well I was even more excited about Carter's and I future. She seemed like she would be the best mother in law, ever. She came across genuine, humble, and down to earth.

Being that this was my first place I didn't know

to cook but wanted to try and impress his mother and father in law. The last thing I wanted to do was keep getting takeout food for them. So I decided to impress them and make a home cooked meal for the first time, ever in my life, and why did I do that. Unfortunately, it didn't go according to plan. The chicken was burnt, the noodles where stuck to the pan, and the canned greened beans where expired. There was no telling how long they had been in my mother's cabinet. All I could remember was by the end of the night the pizza man was at the door. Let's just say, there went the first impression.

A Few days later after we exchanged our Christmas gifts, Carter's family left and headed back home. We were both tired because our routines had been broken. It was time for us both to get back to work. His leave time was ending and my vacation was over.

Meeting his family was a breath of fresh air. We were in need of getting our house back to ourselves and getting back to enjoying life and each other's company again.

I was at work when my phone rang. It was Carter.

"I got it babe, I got it." He excitedly yelled through the phone.

"You got what?" I asked confused. Being up all night watching TV he is known for ordering everything off the infomercials. So, I thought that he ordered something else. That dam TV was going to be the cause of bankrupt for him! I thought to myself. Hell the Fed Ex man knew him personally by name.

"The Total gym equipment! They finally sent it and I'm setting it up now!" He sounded so happy and I felt relieved. "Ok, babe I'll see it when I get home, I get off at eight. So I'll see you soon." I told him mirroring his excitement. "What's for dinner?" he asked?

"Well I don't feel like cooking so let's go out." I told him.

"Sounds good to me babe." He said.

"Let's meet up at the bar or should I come home first and we ride together?" I asked.

"I'll meet you." He said!

A few hours later we met at this bar that was known for having good food.

We became known regulars there and big tippers so, we were always fed extra stiff cocktails with a few extra wings on the side. It was a great place to listen to good music and dance. I can't say it was a good place to relax because it could get fairly ratchet at times. A few people have been shot in and outside the club. So, we never stayed to long. We relaxed, talked had a few cocktails and danced for about an hour.

I kept thinking to myself maybe tonight would be good for me to finally sit down and talk to Carter about the whole James situation, with the AIDS scare. I just had to find the right moment. The music was blaring good music so we danced a few songs back to back. After we busted a few moves on the dance floor, and couple songs later my legs felt weak and I had started to get tired. We were both starting to feel our alcohol as we couldn't keep our hands off each other. I looked down at my watch and seen it was past time to go! He was now on his fifth beer, and sixth shot. Not that I was keeping count or anything.

I couldn't help but notice the drinks had him feeling himself, he seemed a little more upbeat after all he was smiling non stop and I liked this side of him.

He needed this after all he has been through lately.

I knew I was going to have to be the designated driver at the rate he was going but we'd both drove our own cars.

"Babe I'm driving". I demanded.

"Hell no. I'm good so let's go." He told me while leaving a tip.

We got home and he went to the bathroom. I went to the bedroom and took my shoes off. Those heels where killing my feet. At that point I started feeling the cocktails, and the room started spinning so I sat down on the bed to set his alarm clock. I changed my mind about talking to him about tonight, I decided to wait until morning when we both sober up. As soon as I laid down I heard his cell phone ring from the night stand so, I picked it up and yelled, Babe "Mi-Mi calling you." He came in the room, and had a strange look on his face. By the look he gave, I felt like I just missed something major." What's wrong, babe?" He didn't answer nor did he look at me! "Babe, what's on your mind?" I asked as I stood up to hand him the phone.

"You're going to leave me. That girl ant nothing to me." He told me while snatching the phone out of my hand.

"What are you talking about?" I asked him still confused I started walking out the bedroom into the living room when he ran behind me, pushing me through the glass table that sat in the middle of our living room. The glass shattered, I laid on the floor dazed, confused and shocked. I was frightened not knowing what the hell he was going to do next, as I didn't see this coming.

He then slapped me in the face and punched me in the head, catching me off guard. My head swung to the side. "Carter I yelled why did you do that? Why are you doing this to me?"

"You are not going to leave me, he said while chocking me. "What are you talking about?" I started to scream and try to get away from him but he was way too strong.

He then reached over and picked up the total gym and started coming towards me. I had no chance of getting up or moving when I realized what he was about to do with it.

I balled up in fetal position and held my head tight attempting to shield it. He beat the hell out of me as I laid in the middle of the floor in a fetal position helpless, protecting myself because I didn't want to take a blow to the head. He continued to hit me with it repeatedly and then eventually threw it down to the ground. All I could do is try and crawl away towards the door. I was dripping in blood and could barely see as my vision was blurred.

I tried to get up, I cried "Why? Why are you doing this to me? What did I do to you Carter?"

He grabbed the back of my head gripping my hair in his palms and threw me against the wall head first. It felt like minutes that he stood over me as I laid their helpless. Soon after he left the room I ran out of the bedroom towards the door as fast as I could without looking back. The only thing I was concentrating on was getting to the door and getting the hell out of there. I didn't know who this man was. Even the look in his eyes were unfamiliar. "Where the hell you think you going?" He yelled from behind me.

"You ant going nowhere!" He yelled while he had a hand full of hair in his hand.

"Carter, please why are you doing this to me? Please stop! I'll do anything" I yelled and pleaded as I cried in pain. I was mentally and physically hurt and caught off guard.

We locked eyes as he turned to go towards the kitchen. He was mumbling under his breath but I couldn't make out what he was saying. He then sat in the middle of the black and white checkered floor and began stabbing himself. I could not believe what the hell I was witnessing and more so what he was doing to himself. I thought it was a bad dream as I stood there in disbelief with my mouth and eyes wide open. I was scared. I didn't want to move or react not knowing what his reaction would be. I wanted to continue running out the door, but he was no longer focused on me, he was about to kill himself. He was plunging the knife in and out of his leg, and then he started in on his left hand.

I didn't see this coming! There was blood flying everywhere.

"No, please stop baby! What are you doing" I yelled. I was in pain from the beating that I just received from the man that I thought loved me. I didn't know if I was more mentally scared or physically abused at this point.

"You can't leave me! I messed up and I know it! I'm sorry Storm! I'm sorry! I really messed up! "! He was crying harder than ever before, and pleaded for me to stay. He was bleeding profusely. There were blood spots and stains on the floor, all over his shirt and pants. There was even blood splattered on the ceiling. It looked surreal like a crime scene. The knife was slinging everywhere. I didn't know his next move but I did know I had to get that knife from him before he did any further harm.

I ran over to him without thinking and grabbed his arm. I couldn't standby watching him continue doing that to himself so I knew I had to stop him at all cost. I just could not allow it. "What the heck are you thinking? Why are you doing this to yourself? I screamed. "Are you freaking crazy or what? Why are you doing this"? I was so afraid. However, I couldn't show him in that moment.

Not knowing what to do I just reacted not thinking

I gripped his hand tight and snatched the knife from the handle. He then grabbed my legs and hugged me around my knees squeezing as tight as he could.

"I didn't mean to do this babe"! He yelled and cried..

I just stood there trying to take it all in feeling dazed and confused to say the lease. All I could do is replay what just happened. This was unexpected and unlike him. In a matter of minutes, we went from drinking, dancing and having a blast to coming home, him hitting and beating me with a total gym, and stabbing himself. What the hell kind of nightmare was this I thought to myself? Life with him seemed so unpredictable anymore. This was an uneasy feeling as he was not previously like this. I didn't know what to do or where to turn or know if we would ever return his normal self again. This was not the man that I met and fell in love with, nor was I ready to walk away from him.

He even looked and sounded different from his norm and I had no explanation for it.

I was lost for words and scared because I never

seen that look in his eyes. I've never even seen this side of him period. It seemed like it was him in the physical presence but not mentally. I don't think I can ever wrap my head around it or explain it and sound normal.

The next morning when I Woke up I couldn't believe that last night was real. It had to be real because my neck was sore and my back and legs where swollen. He was sleep on the couch when I woke up. I had a headache that I just couldn't shake. I hesitantly went to the restroom to get some medicine from the medicine cabinet when I just so happened to look in the mirror that's when my situation got real and reality set in real quick! Reality hit me, he beat the hell out of me for no reason and I didn't even get a chance to tell him about James, I wonder what would have happened then. The thought alone scared the hell out of me and sent chills through my body!

NEW YEAR'S EVE FROM HELL

It was the Eve of New Year's and I didn't know if I was more excited about us taking off and getting away from our routine lives, or the fact he had planned the whole weekend getaway for us to regroup, and without my help. The thought alone was very mature in nature, sweet, and kind of him. Lord knows I was in desperate need of some relaxation. Especially after all the recent drama, and the ups and downs that had transpired these last few months. I was looking forward to a New Year and new start moving forward especially after his episode! We needed this time to get away and reconnect.

He was still apologizing and wanted so badly to redeem himself, and try and put a smile back on my face. Lately he had been showering me with more gifts, attention and was a little more tentative to my needs. He boasted full of pride nonstop about how much we were going to enjoy ourselves and he was going to make it up to me this weekend. I can't even lie I was kind of excited to see what he had planned for us since he kept bragging.

We rode down to Cincinnati about forty-five minutes away to go party at the Ritz night club. A few of his friends and military buddies followed us down. We actually had four car loads. Before we went to the hotel we stopped off at his cousin Earl house. He was in a fraternity up at UC so of course we had to stop by and turn up early.

They had all types of liquor and beer everywhere. The place was huge! I'd never seen a house like it. I glanced over to my side there sat a pool table in the middle of the living room with Trophies and Alpha Phi Alpha Greek memorabilia everywhere. It felt as if I was in a twilight zone. I saw Alpha paddles, seat covers, picture frames, cups, wall paper, you name it they had it! You could tell that they loved their fraternity. No rush to take a seat as you could take several. There were oversized couches everywhere! When I went upstairs all I could remember is there being a lot of bedrooms and they were all uniquely the same with the decor.

"How many people stay in this dam house" I asked as he gave us a tour.

"It depends on that day cause. Everyday a different frat stays over." He answered as he chuckled.
I was the only female in the house and I felt pretty comfortable so this was cool I thought. A few cocktails and smoke sessions later I was ready to go have some more fun.

"Are we going to get dressed anytime soon because yawl seem to be getting a little too comfortable? I asked.
I had to plant that seed or else we would be here all night and I was ready to go. Shortly after, we headed to the hotel to shit, shower, shave and get dressed for our night out on the town. Carter had reserved three rooms at the Sheraton So that everyone could fall where they lay once we got back from clubbing!

Everyone got Fly, flashy, and fresh. We were ready for

the club in no time, surprisingly! We all met down in the lobby to take pictures before we headed out. Whenever all of us get together we always act a fool and have a good time. Carter and I did not want to drive so we rode with his cousin. Earl is known for keeping a decked car. This time he drove a Chevy with the rims bigger than the car, banging speakers, with white leather seats, and a dam chandelier in the ceiling. Let's just say it's an experience riding with him and racing with the others down I-75. If my hair wasn't sowed in I would have lost it on the highway somewhere, as fast he was driving. Lets just say he lives a little on the adventurous side. He was going so fast that it frightened the mess out of me so I was holding on to the door praying because I didn't want to see it coming. Whatever it may be!

By the time we got to the club let's just say all of us were on one, turned all the way up! I don't even know how we made it but we did and I was so happy to get out that car alive! It felt like I left my ear drums back at the hotel, his speakers are for competition not the dam back seat of a car. But we had a ball. I have to say, Cincinnati knows how to party.

Out of nowhere I started feeling sick. I forgot I was supposed to be taking it easy because I had fibroid surgery the other day. Besides, I was still physically sore from when he had his last episode. Knowing what I was supposed to be doing and actually doing what the doctored ordered was two different things. I wanted to spend this time with Carter and work on our relationship and the issues that we had, that was priority to me.

When we got back to the hotel I took a shower, and laid down to watch T.V., It couldn't have been five minutes after I dozed off. Carter came in the room and slammed the door with a furious look on his face.

"Babe lets go over to the other room, they are in there playing truth or dare!" Carter demanded.

"Truth or Dare for what I asked?" The last thing I wanted to do was entertain, play games or be around people to be honest.

"Come on let's just go for a little while."

"I really don't feel like it, I don't feel so good. Please!" Carter, I thought you would understand considering I've had all these procedures done. The doctors have me on all types of medication but I wanted get out the house and do this for us. "

"I'm not trying to hear that girl get your ass up. Come on let's go!" He demanded.

"Boy bye are you serious? I don't feel good."

"Did you hear me" he yelled not taking no for an answer.

It frightened me and I didn't know how to respond because it caught me off guard. I looked up at him, but before I could say anything else he picked up the wooden chair to the desk and beat the hell out of me with it. I balled up in fetal position on the bed and covered my head. I didn't have a chance in hell to get away. I was in shock that this was really happening to me, again.

Why are you doing this to me again, Carter? I cried between the beatings. Stop, stop. Please stop Carter! I screamed.

Why the hell was this man beating me? After a while he stopped hitting me and I managed to get outside the door. I crawled as fast as I could. I couldn't move my left leg and my arms hurt because they were bruised by me trying to shield myself. When I finally got to the elevator I looked back and seen that he was quickly approaching. My whole body was in pain, I felt it all over.

We got inside the elevator, he kept pacing back and forth. I helpless laid on the ground hoping he did not stump me again. Only the lord knows I couldn't stand another blow. "Bitch I should of killed you!" He told me as blood was dripping down my arm from the blows that I received.

The elevator door opened and I crawled to the desk as fast as I could asking where the pay phones where. The front desk clerk starred at me in awe. You could tell she was wondering what was going on. At that point, the manager on duty came over and asked if I was ok?

"Is there something I can help you with ma'am? Would you like for me to call the police? The manager asked me with concern in his voice.

Carter stood closely behind me and said no sir, she will be ok. He lifted me up to my feet. I was in so much pain but I did not want to bring any further attention to myself. The last thing I wanted was for them to call the police so I dealt with it. The clerk said, the pay phones are over there and pointed towards the corner. I then called my mom. Hoping and praying that she picked up the phone as if my life depended on it.

"Ma! I need you to come get me" I cried as soon as she picked up.

"What's wrong baby?" She asked in a concerned voice.

I looked over at him, not wanting to answer. But I reluctantly told her that He beat me!

"He did what!" She asked in a surprised high pitch voice.

This is the first that my mom had heard of this as I managed to keep it from her the couple times before.

She said, "Where is he at?"

"Right here." I told her.

"Put him on the phone now!" She yelled in a pissed off voice.

I handed the phone to him and stood over in the corner beside the magazine stand.

I don't know what she said as all I heard was her yelling, and him saying yes ma'am. When he hung up he said lets go.

"Let's go where?"

"I'm taking you home. He yelled."

I was afraid and did not want to get in the car with him. I could barely walk so I went to the car and waited while he went back to the room to pack up our bags.

My mind was racing, I was scared at the thought that he would kill me on the way home. I put on my seat belt but kept thinking if I should keep it off just in case I had to jump out. No telling what this man was capable of doing and I didn't want to stick around to find out.

Once he got in the car and looked over at me shaking his head. We then sped off and left skid marks and smoke in the road. We jumped on the highway and I couldn't help but keep looking over at the speedometer. The speed limit was 65 and he was going 86. I kept thinking to myself well if we get pulled over maybe they can take me home. At least I'll get there safe. The whole ride home was silent. He did not say a word. I was quiet because I was thinking of a way to escape from him if he happen to flip out again on the ride home.

I cried just replaying back memories in my head of what just happened. I was confused and shocked as to why he was doing this. I questioned myself over and over. But I knew I'd once again not do anything to provoke him. He was simply just mentally unstable sometimes, and at any moment he could flip without warning. I was scared. I just could not figure it out. He was not the man that I met and fell in love with. I did not know this man at all!

After what seemed like forever later, we arrived to mommies house. I don't think I let the car pull all the way up in the drive way before I jumped out. I ran in the house, right past my mother. She was angrily standing in the door.

"Just where do you think you're going?" She asked.

"Come here let me see your dam face." She said in a stern but concerned voice."

She grabbed me by my chin and turned my face to the side. It was then that Carter walked through the front door. The first thing he said was" I'm sorry Ms. Darlene."

"Oh no you ant sorry, look at what you did to my baby" she unsympathetically said in disbelief.

Before I knew it my mother had sprung over at him, picked him up and threw him against the wall. Now how her little self-had the strength to pick up this two hundred plus solid man I can't tell you. I stood there shocked, and amazed. I felt like I was watching a movie play out in slow motion because I didn't know what was about to happen.

He just stood there defenseless like he knew he was wrong.

She said "now we going to take a trip to the hospital and you're going to pay for it Carter. Do you hear me?" She yelled.

"Well Yes Ma'am" he replied in a low voice with his head held down.

We went to the hospital and the doctors kept asking questions. They were in suspense as to who put they hands on me. I made up a story about getting in a fight with someone I knew I had to support my bruises. The last thing I wanted was for them to call the police or get him in trouble with the military, as I knew his career would be on the line.

Ma'am have you been abused or in an abusive relationship?" the nurse curiously asked.

While looking at both me and Carter with skepticism.

"No I calmly answered"

"Can you just give me some medicine so I can try and lay down, sleep, and just forget about it. "

My mother stood there quite.

I knew that if I didn't seem agitated with the lady she would just continue prying in my business, being nosey and asking unnecessary questions about abuse and the last thing I was going to do was tell her anything.

When we got back to the house I went to sleep because they had given me pain medication to help with comfort. The medication they prescribed me came right on time. Otherwise I would not have been able to sleep because my mind would not stop racing back and forth.

A few hours later I awoke to the smell of breakfast food, I heard laughter coming from the kitchen. When I entered in the kitchen there sat Carter and my mother at the table eating.

"I thought I heard him laughing," I said allowed.

I had no understanding why he was still here.

Not only was he still here but he and my mother were sitting there having breakfast. She actually cooked.

From the looks of it she had cooked them bacon,

sausage, grits, eggs and cup of coffee. I couldn't believe my eyes. I mean didn't this brother just beat me I thought to myself. He immediately stood up when he glanced over at me, and pulled the seat out for me to sit down next to him.

"Are you okay Storm" mommy asked.

Carter said how do you feel baby? I just looked at him with the one eye I could see out of as the other had swollen shut black, purple and blue. My head was hurting worse now. I had to go lye back down.

He followed me back to the room.

"Storm, I need to talk to you." He said in a soft whisper.

I knew that something was mentally wrong with him because he would be one way and a instant later within a blink of an eye he would turn into someone different, someone I didn't know without warning. But no matter what he said or did we still managed to work it out, and crawl back to each others good graces. There was a bond between the two of us that could not break. I can't explain it nor can I say that I've ever felt this way before.

STOLEN JEWELS

Our on one day, off the next day relationship was starting to take a toll on my mental state. It was draining my energy and starting to suck the life out of me as I started to feel like our relationship was coming to a dead end. Something felt different, and I was on edge. I started to think I was going crazy after all of what's been going on lately.

The countdown began. I was growing more anxious by the day because, one thing for sure I couldn't press pause on this thing called life, not even if I wanted to. It was two weeks before Carter was due to deploy.

Iraq was unfortunately, in his near future, even though I prayed only the man upstairs knows if Carter will return home safely! All I could do was frequently send in a prayer, and impatiently wait on him to go and return. Lately, I've been a little beside myself! My nerves were shot to hell as I've been on edge, couldn't sleep, and I was sitting on pens and needles.

He on the other hand, was nervous of course but he was acting out so to speak. He wanted to party every day like it was his last. If he wasn't in somebody's club or bar then he sat and played video games for hours and would get drunk like no other. During this time for example if the house burnt down he wouldn't care. As long as he had his video game, booze, and cigars he was okay.

One night while watching him get his deployment gear together we were having a casual conversation when out of the blue I blurted out to him;

"Babe if something where to happen to you, like you came back with a missing limb an arm, or leg I would still be here for you."

He said. "If my shit get blown up I ant coming back, I'll off myself first. They'll be sending me back to the states in a box."

I stood there shocked, and caught off guard as I was not expecting for him to say something like that. Here I was trying to comfort and console him and he went off on a tangent and somewhere else with the conversation.

"Why would you say some crazy crap like that Carter?" I asked in a serious tone.

"You think I'm kidding he said in a jokingly manner. I ant gone live like that!"

I was mind blown, and couldn't believe he said that. I grew even more concerned about him in that instant. All I could think about was him, his mental state, and what was going on in his head. On the other hand I couldn't stop thinking about what was going to happen with us and our relationship. After all he was due to deploy again and soon. It started to stress me out? Was he coming back, I thought? Did he have everything he needed? I couldn't help but think what it was going to be like living every day without him. He was due to deploy for six month at a minimum. What was it going to be like for him living in the desert, with the sand storms and all? Hell I hadn't been without him for years so this was going to be a new venture. I didn't know what was to come of all of this but I did know that I had to keep myself occupied!

I knew picking up additional classes, more like twenty one credit hours, and working fifty hours a week would keep my mind occupied. I thought a motivating factor for myself would be focusing on the Dean's list, something positive and would be beneficial to my future!

Being that we weren't married, I didn't feel comfortable living on base without him while he was deployed. Our relationship was rocky, and he was distant. When I say distant we were under the same roof but it felt like we were a millions miles away mentally. I decided that in order for me to see where this man is trying to take our relationship, I would have to take a step back in hopes of moving forward with our future. This was a risk that had high stakes but it was a risk worth taking. So I thought!

Being engaged was not enough, and setting a date seemed like the last thing on his mind. I'm marriage material so, I felt that I had to take him out of his comfort zone and move out. I had to show him better than I could tell him. It took everything out of me to do it but I felt it had to be done, more so to test the status of our future together. Because at this point I was clearly uncertain.

When he awoke the next morning I got up with him to see him off. He had to get his dose of me before work as usual. As soon, as he left I jumped in the shower, and then began packing. I had a nine a.m. reservation to pick up the U-Haul. But I knew I had to make the best of my time because I wanted to be gone before he came home for lunch. I didn't want to leave this man and Lord knows I love him but I just had that gut feeling that if I stayed he would remain comfortable and violent. If I was here when he came home, and he caught me trying to leave, ant no dam telling what the hell would happen. His deployment was coming so fast and I was about to be left here with more questions than answers. Every time I attempted to talk with him about it he blow me off. Not to mention we couldn't get pregnant. We had been trying for years. The issue kept surfacing considering his son died a few years back, in a previous relationship. He felt like time was ticking and I couldn't give him what he wanted. This made me feel less than average as a women. He had been very passionate and determined about getting me pregnant. He was pressuring me to replace the son that he lost. That was a huge weight on my shoulder and a burden to face. I knew that it was not a good time for me to get pregnant and on top of that I knew that I had to finish school. So, we split!

It had been only a few days now since I moved off base. I was in desperate need to get my own apartment and become more independent as a women. You know, stand on my own two feet and be more self-sufficient. I had to let him know that I was capable of doing it and further more I had to do it for myself. Hell, for years all I did was worry about him and neglecting my own needs. In the matter of three days I made moves that I did not know I was capable of. I was able to walk away from this violent and empty relationship and focus strictly on school. At least for now to be honest I shocked myself. My thought of leaving him and the actual move seemed like it happened so quickly. Even though I left and moved, my heart was still there. He had my heart and always will.

I found time to secretly find an apartment, sign the lease, and move in. I felt there was no need for me to continue living on base and he was due to deploy shortly. I had to show him now or he would never see that I was no longer going to make myself available to him. I was taking a walk out on faith because he had me spoiled since I left mommy's house initially. So, I was about to turn a new leaf. I didn't need him to take care of me it's just something that he wanted to do. Being that I've always worked and had my own he wanted me to feel as if I needed him. It was a good feeling. I never had a father to show me such love. It didn't matter how much the man showered me with gifts, I knew I had to make a move.

I went and picked up the U-Haul and when I came back there was a truck there already moving the military family across the street. Their truck was more like a 75 footer, and my U-Haul was 20 feet. I parked the truck near the back entrance of the door close to the garage so I could easily transport my things. I had my brothers helping me move. My little ass didn't feel like picking up couches, beds or anything else for that matter but I had to get the job done, heels and all.

I was moving stuff faster than a crack head on the move. I was on a mission and didn't want any drama.

I was so much in a rush I didn't even bag my clothes up. I threw my clothes on the truck just any kind of way. I really didn't care just as long as they were on there. Time was just not on my side. I looked down at my watch realizing that time had gotten past me. I only had thirty minutes before he was due home for lunch. So, I was cutting it close I had to turn up, turbo speed. You never know how much stuff you have until it's time to move. I was just throwing everything on the truck. The last thing I needed was for him to catch me trying to leave. He would kick my ass and probably kill me for leaving him.

We got done with a few minutes to spare and I locked up the house and left the keys in the mailbox. My brother drove the truck and I jumped in my car which was parked in the garage. In front of the garage was that moving truck blocking my car from pulling off. This time there were no driver, or movers to be found. I instantly grew pissed off as now was not the time for this. I had to get out of here before Carter returned home. I jumped back out the car and went walking around the side walk looking for the movers to move their truck so that I could leave on time. There was no sign of anyone. For the first time ever no one was outside. Damn! I yelled at the top of my lungs. I didn't have time for this! I went back to the garage and stared at my Riviera. There were dents on both sides. What the hell! I don't know if I was more upset about the damage or the fact that I had ten minutes before he was due back home.

My car was sitting there shining nice and pretty. I jumped in the car after looking around again and there was still not a soul to be found. I started the car and thought twice about taking it but I had no choice. I looked at the clock and could only image what he would do to me. I pulled off slow I scraped the left hand side of the car on the wall of our garage. No, No, No, I screamed while hitting the steering wheel and dash board.

"Darn it! I yelled."

I threw the car in reverse to try and go backwards. It was then I hit the other side of my car. I just sat there pissed. Not wanting to get out and look at the damage. I knew it was bad, but didn't know how bad so I instantly felt sick to my stomach as I could only image the damage that's been done. At that point I seen two men it was the dam moving company drivers. I started blowing the horn and cursing at them so loud thank goodness my windows were rolled up so they couldn't hear me. I mean I said every word in the book not noticing the back windows were rolled down. Oh well at that point it was too late and I didn't care that they heard me. One of the drivers appeared from nowhere and jumped in and pulled the truck up a little further so I could get out.

I forgot all about Carter coming and me trying to leave. Hell I fucked my car up was all I could think about. When I pulled up to my new apartment, everyone was waiting on me. My brothers and their friends were all starring at my car wondering what the heck happened to it. One minute she was shining nice and pretty and the next minute she came back banged up! "Really!"

When I got out and seen all of the damage to my car I was disgusted! I couldn't believe all the damage that was caused. The back of my car looked like I had got in a middle of two monster trucks the dents were enormous. I was pissed but I couldn't be mad at no one but myself. I just stood there in awl.

"Dam Sis, What happened to your car?" My little brother Sam yelled.

"I told you your behind can't drive my brother Javelle shouted.

Javelle was my middle brother He's always been a know it all with his smart, handsome chocolate self. He owns his own trucking business so you know he had something to say about my driving incident. But now was not the time for that. I was already upset so I didn't want to hear it! Not now.

"What the hell happed to your car girl?" He yelled with his country accent.

"Right now is not a good time. I don't want to talk about it." I screamed.

All I need yawl to do is unload this stuff for me. I said while walking towards the apartment. And if Carter call any of yawl tell him you don't know where I am or that you haven't heard from me today. Is that clear! I said with conviction and authority in my voice. They all just stood there confused and dazed.

I finally got settled in my new apartment but everything felt weird, foreign, and out of place because I had never lived by myself. Now it was just me and my dog Showtime. I was treading on new founded territory. All I could do is take it one day at a time at this point.

But I have to admit minute by minute I was missing
Carter. My phone rang it was him he was finally calling
me. I was nervous. Oh my, what was I going to say? I
thought to myself.

"He said where the fuck are you? Why is all of my
shit gone? What are you doing, Storm?"

I didn't steal anything. If you remember, I paid
half so I left you half of the furniture, and the pool table. I
have no reason to steal from you but I do need something
to sit on when I get home. I told him. "You are getting
ready to deploy Carter and I'm scared. You been acting
different and I knew I had to move out because I feel like
our relationship is at a standstill and your content with
the way we are and I can't settle for that. I've done all I
can. You keep saying were going to get married but when
you're leaving and that's the last thing on your mind. I
cannot allow myself to settle for that. As much as I love
you I have to do what's best for me."

"Where are you girl? Where the hell is my dog?" I
ignored him.

His friend Jamal and I were really close. He would
come over our house every day and sometimes spend the

night. Often times he would bring his fiancé and everyone hung out and kicked it at our house. I guess everyone considered our house the kicking it spot, except for me! I was cool with a visit or two but it was becoming draining and a bit too much. I considered Jamal like a little brother he was a go to person for me when I needed advice about Carter considering they are best friends. Jamal was a very large guy. He weighed about three hundred pounds, at least 6 feet tall, buff black and not so cute guy from California. He and his fiancé were expecting, so he was very excited about his unborn daughter. As his friend for the last three years I was excited for them. One late summer eve, I'll never forget it, August 28, shortly after I'd left Carter, I was blindsided by Jamal.

I was still trying to get settled in my apartment. It had only been a few days now although I was still missing the hell out of Carter. I was refusing to call him. Lord knows I wanted to but I didn't. My pride was getting the best of me. I had to remind myself why I left in the first place. As I moved out for a reason and I wanted it to stay that way. But in the back of my mind I knew his birthday was coming and he was due to deploy soon.

That's all I could think about. I tried to keep myself busy and make my apartment feel cozy and comfortable considering it was my first apartment on my own. But it was nothing compared to the large space I was use to in the Base housing with Carter. I was beginning to see how much luxury I had.

But it did feel weird because I was not use to Carter not being by my side. Nor was I use to use to waking up without him. What I was use to was him being there every day and night. It had been years since I slept alone and I refused to start now so I was sleeping on the couch as I found comfort there. It wasn't too big and was small enough to hold me and the dog.

After watching fear factor I suddenly dozed off when my phone rang. I jumped up and reached for my phone, I looked over at the clock and it was about 1:15 in the morning. I was startled out of my dam sleep. Who in the hell? I thought to myself? I looked at my caller I.d. It was Jamal. Why was he calling me so late, something had to of been wrong, I thought.

"I decided to answer and why did I do that?!" That phone call changed my life forever and not for the good!

"Hello, Storm. What's up you awake?" He asked. "No, boy what's wrong, why the hell are you calling me this late? This better be important" I said sounding irritated and half sleep.

"I'm downtown leaving the club. I'm so drunk. I don't think I'm going to be able to make it home Storm."

"Well what do you want me to do?" I asked.

"Can I come over your house and sleep this off for a couple of hours and leave early in the morning?" He asked sounding extremely drunk.

"No Jamal! Where is your fiancé I asked?" He told me that she went out of town visiting family, and that he didn't want to risk driving on base getting a DUI. I hesitantly said ok, and gave him the address so that he could come over for a couple hours. Moments after we hung up I jumped up and went into my bedroom to get him a few pillows and some linen. I had to put my jogging pants underneath my night gown. By the time I laid it on the couch he was knocking at the door. Dam that was fast I thought to myself. He reeked of marijuana and booze. I told him that if he needed to jump in the shower he was more than welcome to, but I also stressed to him that I really wasn't comfortable because if Carter was to come over or find out that he slept over my house there would be problems as he wouldn't have any understanding.

"You know this is not a good look so try to leave as soon as you can ok?"

"I know Storm I don't need any problems." He told me in slurred words.

"Good Night Jamal, and If you leave before I get up in the morning just lock the door on your way out." He said ok and went to lay on the couch. I really felt uncomfortable because I had never been around him without Carter's presence. I allowed him to sleep on my couch and I went and lied in my bed. The couch had been my bed but I guess a few hours wouldn't hurt. I tossed and turned all night, knowing that there was someone sleeping in my living room but somehow I finally dozed off.

It was about 9:15 am when I woke up to Jamal sitting on my bed rubbing my legs up and down slowly and it looked as if drool and slobber was running out of his mouth. I thought I was dreaming.

When I realized it was really happening.

I slapped his hand away and tried to push him off me as hard as I could. "What the fuck are you doing?" I screamed as I hopped up. He began to press his weight on me and pent my arms above my head. I couldn't believe it.

"Get the fuck off of me! Stop what the fuck are you doing?" I screamed as loud as I could while kicking and screaming. He began groping me.

"You know you want me storm so stop playing like you don't." Sweat was rolling off of him and on to me and I was grossed out trying to squirm away and get his big ass off of me at the same time.

"Carter don't love you, he said! That dude has been cheating on you for years. You need to give me a chance." He told me while still trying to kiss my neck. "Yeah baby girl I've been having my eye on you since I met you, girl!

"What the fuck! Get off of me Jamal" I continued yelling and screaming Help somebody, help! I cried.

"Shut the fuck up!" he yelled and slapped me in the face.

He then tore my jogging pants off and threw himself on top of me and began grouping, and touching me he eventually raped me, took my since of pride and dignity with him. I was in shock and could not believe that he was actually forcing himself on me.

"Who would have ever thought he'd do this?" I was terrified, and did everything in my power to get him to stop and get off of me. I was screaming, punching him and kicking as hard as I could but it did not faze his big ass. He was about two hundred and eighty five pounds or so. I was crying profusely and couldn't stop screaming in hopes of my neighbors hearing me. But my cries went unheard and no one came to my rescue. In that moment, I flashed back to when my cousin raped me while babysitting me. I was eight. I blacked out and when I regained my composure I couldn't help but notice he was still in me. When he was done he wiped his sweat off with my night gown, and started walking toward the door when he turned around and said.

"Now if you tell anybody bitch I will kill you!" As soon as I heard my door close I ran to lock it and sat in the corner for hours in disbelief, crying, screaming, and rubbing my legs, rocking back and forth. So many questions filled my head. What was I going to do? Why did he do this? How could he do this to me? Then I thought how was I going to tell Carter? All I could do is cry. I sat in the shower for hours trying to scrub the dirt away. I felt betrayed, dirty, taken advantage of, abused, battered, and confused. I had never known that he liked me, and what would make him want to throw his military career away? All the unanswered questions and thoughts that continued racing threw my mind. I was speechless and I didn't see this coming!

Later that day there was a knock at the door I was scared to answer, so I didn't. My phone started ringing again, but I didn't answer. After a few minutes it continued so I decided to go look out of the peephole and it was Jade. She was beating on the door as if she was the police. Only a few people knew where I lived but I was scared it was Jamal coming back. I opened the door with a knife and grabbed her up in case he may have been behind her. When I looked down the balcony I seen Jamal car parked outside my apartment, he blew at me and smiled. "Oh My God!"

He's back I screamed as I slammed the door.

"Who is back" she said, looking confused. I busted out in tears. "What's wrong Storm? She asked.

"I don't know how to put this or even if I should tell you. He said if I told anyone he would kill me. I live alone now I'm scared I can't. I don't want anything else to happen." What are you talking about, Storm? Calm down, what's wrong?" She asked.

Tears continued flowing down my cheeks faster than I could wipe. I didn't know where to begin so I just started crying harder and harder trying to find a way to tell her, and find the words to say. After what felt like minutes I finally was able to get it out, and it felt like such a weight lifted off my shoulders.

"What! She yelled in disbelief. She immediately picked up the phone. "We have to call the police."

"Hang up please no, don't do that."

"That animal need to be locked up, somewhere girl! She told me. "Oh shit girl, what about Carter did you tell him?" She said with a dead stare in her face not blinking as if she couldn't wait for my response.

"No, and you can't tell him yet either. I told her. "I'm trying to figure all this shit out. I'll be dammed if I do and dammed if I don't did you see him outside I asked? Wait a minute so he came back? Yes, I said he's stalking me. I'm scared and don't know what to do. I feel like a hostage in my own house and I don't even want to answer the dam phone because Jamal keeps calling me. What the hell I screamed? I'm going crazy just thinking about this. I don't know what I'm going to do, or how to tell Carter. I was hurt and broke down crying more.

My phone rang and it was Carter. I instantly started shaking more, and hairs stood up on the back of my neck. I didn't want to answer as I didn't want him to see me like this. But against my better judgment I answered. He said he had just got off work and was on his way over to the house. I didn't want to upset him by telling him that, first of all I let his friend spend the night and second that he raped me. That would automatically set him off. Even though I really didn't want him to come over I told him that it was ok.

Jade looked at me with concern her eyes were big and she was hinging on every word that came out of my mouth.

"So is he coming?" she anxiously asked.

I just gave her the look. Storm she repeated "Is he on his way now? Are you going to tell him?"

I bit my bottom lip and stood there dazed, frightened, and motionless as this was the last conversation I ever thought I would have to have with Carter. How do you tell your fiancé that you were raped by his best friend? When is a good time to tell him that I've been raped when he is forty-eight hours from deployment and his birthday is tomorrow? How did this happen? What was I to do? I started pacing the floor wrecking my brain on what to say.

"Should I stay or should I go? Jade asked. I looked at her and I heard her but I didn't respond. I stood there and speechless. I was still trying to take it all in. A few minutes later, she said, "Look girl I love, you but I think this is a conversation that you need to sit down and have with him one on one. I think I'm going to go ahead and head on home but if you need me please don't hesitate to put me on speed dial, Sis." She demanded.

I didn't want to get her involved so I hugged my friend and sent her on her way. But in the back of my mind I was hesitant because who knows how he is going to react. This could very well set him off on one of his episodes. I was beyond scared, and my mind drew a blank when I thought about the conversation that I was about to have.

A few minutes later there was a knock at the door. I instantly started shaking because I didn't know if it was Jamal or Carter. Either way I was about to be in uncomfortable territory. I looked out the peephole and seen it was Carter so I opened the door. He stood there in full uniform, with a smile on his face until he saw the expression on my face.

"What's wrong baby?" He asked me as he reached to give me a hug. I punched him and pushed him off of me. He caught me off guard and I was not aware of what I was doing. I guess it was a reaction to him coming to close in my space. I had a temporary flash back.

"What the fuck! What's up with you Storm?"

Talk to me babe what's going on?"

I reached to wipe my tears away, when he gently grabbed me by my wrists. I broke down in tears. He knew something was up as I'd never done that before. For moments I stood there speechless not able to find the words to say, or know how to tell him I had been raped!

"Why are you acting like this?" He asked.

I looked at him and instantly broke down crying. "You know I'm leaving in two days get yourself together man I want to celebrate my birthday with you Storm, before I go. He told with concern and sadness in his voice. "You know I'm leaving. All I want to do is be with you baby cause I'm actually afraid this time. I'm scared to go."

I just looked away and couldn't help but sob more.

"Baby come here talk to me what's up?" He, sincerely asked as he reached for my waist. He tried kissing me on my neck and for some reason I still smelled Jamal. I instantly began to cry harder. My stomach started to cringe and felt like it was tied in knots. Honestly, I didn't know what to do, but one thing was certain I couldn't hold back anymore! I had to be honest and tell him. I knew I had to let him know but I was scared of how he would react as I knew this would probably be a trigger point for him. "What the heck is wrong with you Storm? Talk to me baby." I couldn't find the words to say nor did I know where to start.

"He rapped me." I uttered in a faint voice.

He looked at me in disbelief and started asking questions after question without allowing me to answer then he paused for a second and yelled by who? I then looked at him, and stood there in total silence while looking him in his eyes. For what felt like eternity.

"It was Jamal!" I quietly uttered.

"Jamal who!" He asked.

My best friend?" He said while looking at me with the most evil eyes.

Before I could respond. He jumped over my counter towards the knives. While he was still in midair something internally told me to get the hell out of there so, I dashed for the door. I was scared and wasn't about to stick around to see what he was about to do next.

All I saw was red as I ran down the stairs, and across the lawn as fast as I could. I was barefoot and all, but I felt I was running for my life. I looked back and notice he was close behind. I couldn't believe I was running and he was actually chasing me with a knife. I started beating on my friend Ashley door and right when she answered the door he had held the knife up to me ready to Plunge me with it. Thank God, Ashley opened the door before he had a chance to do anything. I slammed the door and fell on her floor. "Unable to catch my breath and still trying to realize what the hell just happened.

Girl, what is going on?" She asked.

I was too out of breath from running to respond. All I wanted to do was catch my breath. I was so happy to have made it, and felt blessed to be alive. I tried to gather my breath and ask for her phone all while crying and shaking at the same time.

"I need to call my mother, where is your phone?"

Ashley said "Why is Carter at my door acting like a crazy man?

What happened and do I need to call the police?"
She frantically asked.

"I need your phone can I please use your phone." I
yelled.

Hell I knew it could get ugly and I didn't know
what his reaction would be but I didn't think he would
have reacted that way. I didn't do anything wrong dam I
yelled!

Minutes later my mother showed up at Ashley house to
pick me up. She asked why I didn't call and tell her about
me getting raped. She was crying with me, holding me
tight trying to console me and make me feel safe.
Unfortunately with no success.

"Baby I'm sorry" she said in a sobbing voice.

"Carter is on his way to the base looking for Jamal
and I don't know what he is going to do to him, Storm!

Baby, I'm very concerned. It's his birthday and he
is leaving for the war tomorrow. He 's also intoxicated!"

So, I don't want to call the police on him.

"Baby, don't you think we need to call the police
and press charges on Jamal?" Storm. She asked. Did you

hear me?

>After no response she said Storm baby "Come on lets go home."

You've had enough it's okay baby it's time to go! I was scared to leave.

When we got outside I couldn't help but immediately start looking for Carter, he was gone. Then Jamal and he was no where in sight. I have to admit, I was scared to death! Once I got into moms car I looked at my phone I had over eighty missed calls. I couldn't believe it. Carter had blew my phone up and left me numerous messages. He said that he was going to kill Jamal. And that I needed to press charges against him. He also said that he was going to report to his First Shirt. First Shirt is a military liaison between enlisted and officers as well as a disciplinary person. He had to report to the First Shirt because he and Jamal were not going to be able to work together peacefully. They both worked together at the base hospital whenever they come back from deployment. A few hours later Carter came back over to the house ready to talk this time. He had calmed down, just a little bit as had time to think.

All he kept asking is how did he know where you lived? Why was he at your house? How in hell did this happen? All the questions he was asking is what ran through my mind before I even allowed Jamal to come over. I was pissed that he was blaming me! But mad at myself, at the same time scared thinking about Jamal coming back or stalking me. On the other hand I was afraid for what Carter was going to do? I was more so afraid of what was next. The last thing I wanted to do was ruin Carter's birthday!

"I'm calling the police and you are going to press charges on this son of a bitch. I'm not going to allow you be afraid of this Kat! " Do you hear me he yelled?"

He picked up the phone and called the local sheriff office. The whole time I kept thinking to myself that Carter was not going to be here to protect me. That's the only reason I didn't want to call because my life was in danger and I didn't own a gun. Within minutes the sheriff showed up to the door. He was there to investigate and to file a report. The next day I was invited down to the station to speak with the detectives to further investigate and file charges. They made me feel as if I wasn't the victim. They continued to ask me questions over and over and in different ways as if I was going to change my answers. I started to feel more dirty and uncomfortable talking with them and to make matters worse they were two men. I would have been more at ease if there was at least a woman there for comfort. On top of that they treated me like I was the one who rapped him. I was already feeling violated, and they made me feel worse, Making me repeat my story, over and over, and asking the same questions just different ways. I was done with it all. I told my mom they made me not want to tell on anyone or even call the police again especially if you have to be interrogated like that for trying to ask for help. This is ridicules I felt. They made me feel low and dirty all over again. The system shouldn't be set up that way. But who am I to say. I think they should have provided me better resources to protect myself from that animal. Having the no contact stocking order made me feel like I had a piece of paper protecting me from my stalker.

The next day sadly Carter had left for deployment what was I going to do now.

A few weeks had went by when I received a letter to appear in court. I had a court date in the Federal Building. Court was the last place I wanted to be and it was one of the first times I'd ever step foot in one. I was nervous as hell and didn't want to face Jamal again.

I started to get depressed lately and couldn't tell you the last time I slept or ate anything. At this point I know it had been weeks and it was starting to show. I hadn't noticed the weight loss as I didn't look in the mirror anymore. Hell I barely wanted to shower these days. Somehow I had fail into deep despair being that I was alone and living in fear that Jamal was going to come back again. He showed up to court with his military lawyers and I showed up with my family ready to represent myself as a public defender wouldn't be able to do anything for me. I was better off speaking for myself on my own behalf because I didn't meet her until five minutes before court began. I felt it was a losing battle. His conniving ass wore his uniform and attempted to look innocent. I thought to myself only if they knew the animal hiding behind that uniform. This was all a cover up. I was initially scared and intimidated by his presence. This was the first time being in the same room since the day he forever changed my life, when he raped me! I could not afford an attorney so I had one appointed to me. The lawyer asked me about the case two minutes before it was time for court. I was ready to speak on my own behalf without representation but I guess they hired this clown to speak for me. A few weeks later I got a letter in the mail from the courts. They stated based on their findings there was not enough evidence to support my case, and that he could not be criminal charged. However, I could pursue civil litigation. I did not understand how there was not enough evidence to put him in jail but I could sue him for money. I did not want to deal with Jamal or any of this anymore. Although it would be difficult somehow I just wanted to put this all behind me somehow, pick up the pieces, and move on as best I could.

How dare them I said while ripping up the paper! There is not a dollar amount in the world that would give me back my priceless jewels that he helped himself to and stole from me. I didn't want to face him, or be in the same room with him again. I was flabbergasted. I couldn't erase that memory. And the last thing I wanted to do is face him again in court. I just wanted it to be over with. I was done with it and wanted to try my best to put this behind me and pick up the pieces from there.

Carter came back from Overseas and he was more distant than ever it was like I didn't know this man. Hell I wasn't privy to the exact date he came home because he didn't come to me. I was in South Carolina visiting a friend when I found out about his return. My phone rang. I saw his number flash across my caller I.d. I could not believe it. What was he doing calling from his cell phone, I did not know he was back!

"Hello." I answered with confusion and hesitation in my voice.

He sounded excited to hear my voice. "I'm back." He yelled through the phone with excitement in his voice

"You're back where?" I asked very confused.

"I'm in Louisville. Kentucky?"

"What! How long have you been back?" I asked.

He said a few days as if it was nothing.

"Ok, so why am I just now hearing from you?" I asked him with in bafflement.

There was a brief silence on the line? So I broke the awkwardness "Well ok, I'm on my way then" I told him.

"You on your way where?" He asked surprised as if he didn't want me to come.

 "I'm on my way to your grandma house where else would you be when you there besides over your auntie house?" Don't play me I said as I hung up. Something wasn't right with that question, or anything about the conversation. I instantly caught an attitude and was determined to get to the bottom of this. Something didn't seem right. I couldn't get in the car fast enough! I threw my packed bags in the back seat of my convertible and pulled off. Oh shoot I thought to myself. I have to tell my friend that I'm leaving I thought. I shoot him a text message letting him know I left the keys under the mat and I was out! When I jumped on the highway I suddenly noticed the police was out so I knew I had to be cautious. I knew I couldn't afford to get any tickets. The whole time I kept thinking and reminding myself nonstop. I couldn't help but replay the conversation in my head I was all in my feelings so I put the petal to the metal. I didn't give a care in the world until I seen those red and blue lights flashing and heard the police sirens pulling down behind me. Wow I was on cloud nine. I couldn't believe this man! All I had on my mind was getting in front of this man and seeing what the hell he was on as he had obviously lost his dam mind. I was pissed.

The next thing I know I'm getting pulled over with the K-9 dog. A older white officer with a few grayish strings of hair came walking towards me with his slue feet, and dog. I was mad but nervous as hell because I knew that I had one or two joints already rolled in the trunk inside of a stiletto in one those suite cases.

"Ma'am do you know why I'm pulling you over? He asked.

"Yes officer, I do. I have an emergency. I didn't realize I was speeding until seconds before you stopped me sir I apologize.

"May I ask why you are speeding ma'am? Is there something wrong? The nosy officer continued to asked.

"Because my fiancé just got back from war and I have to get to Louisville sir.

"May I see your license and registration?"

"I reached in my orange duffle bag looking purse I couldn't find it because I had all my cash out of the wallet? So, I dumped it all on the seat. I had about five thousand dollars in hundreds, fifty's and twenty's.

"Ma'am May I ask why you have all this money in cash" he asked me in a suspicious way.

"I'm on vacation and visiting friends so I always carry cash wherever I go."

He continued to look me over, and said "Please step out of the car and put your hands on the hood."

"What for sir?" I asked.

"Step out the vehicle while I search for drugs."

Really, officer. I said annoyed. I couldn't believe he thought I was selling or transporting drugs because I have bad credit and paid cash for everything. Minutes later after him and the sniffing dog searched the car wasted his time and found nothing he said you're okay to go. I was still nervous as hell and scared on the inside. But on the outside you couldn't tell it as I remained cocky but more so self-assured. Shortly after, I looked at the clock and seen I had lost time so I remained in a rush to get there. When I pulled off I was speeding so it spit rocks his way hitting him. I didn't give a fuck. It was about five miles down the road I was pulled over again. I knew he radioed in for me to get pulled over so I remained calm and asked how I could help him when he came to the car. "He said ma'am I clocked you going 102 in a 70 mile per hour zone. May I ask why you are speeding?

"Sir I apologize like I told the previous officer my fiancé just got back from Iraq and I'm trying to get to him so can you just give me my ticket so I can get to him?" I told him with an attitude.

"Ma'am we have to make sure that all are safe out here so can you please slow down?" He told me.

"Yes, sir I apologize."

"He said, I'm going to be watching you!"

Ok, sir I replied, nonchalantly. This defiantly put me behind schedule but I had to slow down. When I got to Mohammad Ali Blvd. where his grandparents stayed. The door was shut, blinds where closed and it didn't look like any action was going on so I drove around the back to see if I saw his car. It was there so I drove back around the front and parked. I had to make sure my makeup and lip stick was right before I got out so I double checked the rearview mirror then I sprayed a little perfume to freshen up. I couldn't tell you the last time I seen my man so I had to smell and look good for him even without notice.

I got out and went and knocked on the patio door. It was enclosed so I didn't want to just walk in. I hit on the door harder and called his name. There was no answer. Why in the hell would I drive six hours here, get two speeding tickets, and almost get hauled off to jail for this man to not answer the door. I was pissed, and felt disrespected and couldn't believe he did this to me. So in anger I decided to drive past his father his car wasn't parked there so I did a drive by two of his aunties, and then a cousin house before I jumped back on the highway. He was truly missing in action for real.

I was beyond furious and starting to feel some type of way. The remaining two in a half hour drive to Dayton. I blew his phone up and left him several messages that brought me to the conclusion he wasn't trying to be found. But Why? I asked myself. What the hell was going on.

Later that evening I thought I heard a knock on the door but I wasn't expecting anyone so I continued to ignore it. A few moments later I heard that knock again this time it was louder as if someone was determined to get in. Oh hell I thought to myself. Who is this at my door? I started walking towards the door to look out the peep hole. It was Carter standing there with his head against the door wearisomely listening as if I had someone in here. I really didn't want to answer because he had my ass out there in Louisville looking retarded. So, I wanted to make him feel the same although I didn't have it in me. A few knocks and phone calls later, I decided to hear him out because I had nothing but questions for him once he was done with his spill. The last thing I was doing was listening. He said that he couldn't face me and that he was still upset about everything.

"Look how it all played out before he deployed."
He said.

"I'm still trying to figure out how the hell he knew where you lived, why was he here?

"How did this happen?"

You had my heart Storm and I don't know what to do anymore, I'm confused. For the first time, Storm. The first time he repeated. You hurt me." He cried! You hurt me! He screamed again.

"Carter, I did not do anything to you, to hurt you." I clarified.

"He took something from me that I can't get back. How am I the blame for getting raped? He violated me to the point that I can't sleep, haven't been eating and all I've been worried about is if he was coming back again. The thought alone consumed me, I was fearful that he was coming back and this is no way to live. I have not had anyone to protect me as that piece of paper of a no contact stocking order was not enough. You were overseas so I moved my little brother in with me for protection so I wouldn't be alone. After that all you have to say is that you're hurt? You can't be serious." I yelled.

"I've put my life on hold, and have done nothing but wait on you to come back from overseas so we can pick up where we left off." I could help but get upset at the way he was shifting the blame on me. "You call me and tell me you back, I get two speeding tickets, almost kill myself driving and chance going to jail trying to get to see you. And no one answers the door. If that ant a smack in the face I don't know what is! You've got some explaining to do again what was that about?" I asked.

"I'm sorry babe, I apologize. I never planned for that to happen. He said.
When I got back all the family came over. I was tired, had jetlag and once I got to granny's I fell into a deep sleep." His head was held down in shame or guilt I don't know couldn't tell yet. I guess that was the first thing off the top of his head because that's what it sounded like. How was it that I was the last one to find out that he was back? I knew I caught him lying I but I didn't have proof. If he wasn't lying then he was hiding something from me.

"Well, your apology is not enough Carter! What you done was beyond disrespectful! I don't know how much more of this I'm going to take.

"Babe, I'm sorry." he said.

You've got some major making up to do! You are going to pay those tickets off, take me shopping and dinner for starters." He chuckled and agreed, without hesitation. No problem babe! Before I knew it he had palmed my behind, and pint me against the wall. Let's just say we had to do breakfast because we didn't make it out the house for dinner. Had too much catching up to do!

The next morning he said that being away that long made him put his life in perspective. He said I want a family, I want a son to show him how to survive out here. I want kids to spread my seed and keep my name going. I didn't know where this conversation was coming from or where it was going. He said I just seen some shit and I just don't understand. He broke down in tears.

"Please tell me Carter what did you see?"

I went and kneeled down on the floor holding his head in my arms while he wailed, and wept in tears. I just can't take it, I want to live my life, because I see too much death! You never know when it will end or if it will ever stop and he silenced. I began rubbing his head.

"I think you need to talk to me or someone even a professional maybe. You need to talk with superiors or other personal in the military I know they deal with this type of stuff every day and can give us some resources to help you. You can't deal with it alone. You can't keep this bottled inside. I pleaded."

"You need to let it all out." You can't fight this alone nor should you try! You don't have to. Tell me Carter! I said.

What happened babe?"

He started crying more. Non stop.

"I'm here for you babe. I want to know what you went through, everything you saw "so, I can know how to help you. But only when you're ready.

"I can't talk about it "he said.

"I have nightmares Storm, all I want to do is try and forget about it but I can't.

"That's obviously not the way to go about it Carter, You need help I yelled. If nothing else please open up to me, let me in, so you don't have to go through this by yourself." I pleaded.
"I love you and I hate to see you like this."
 You won't let me in to help with the situation, and it drives me crazy. I want to know everything. Do you know how it feels to know you went to war, and ever since you've returned home for some reason you've changed. It's often feels like you're physically here but mentally somewhere else and your pushing me away. It's almost like you're a shell sometimes. I can't help you because you won't let me. I don't have a clue as to what your experiences are because you refuse to talk to me about it. You shut me out every time I bring it up! It's almost like your using it as a defense mechanism.

NEXT CHAPTER OF LIFE

Carter had been back for a while now. Ever since he'd come back I can't help but notice he returned a different man. He was not the same person I knew before he left. Our relationship was not the same. It felt as if he had resentment towards me for what happened before deployment. The whole rape situation, him losing his temper and snapping trying to stab me, and everything that followed had not yet been settled nor discussed. He was still living in that moment from before he left. He left two days after it all went down. He spent his whole deployment placing the blame on me.

The fact that there were issues behind it and he didn't even want to sit down and talk about it or try and work through it or find a solution was quite troubling to me. He had built up so much anger, and really manifested within him, while he was overseas. He had every right to be upset, but I just couldn't stop from feeling like what about me, and my feelings? I lived through the physical torture I was violated, I was the victim. I had to live with the fact that this animal took something from me that was personal. This man violated me in the worse way possible and he changed my life and how I viewed it. My life was forever changed. He took that from me, which is something that is priceless, intangible and I can't get back. Not only that but he had no understanding that with rape, comes trust issues, and you try and keep from letting others so close. Ultimately, it's a healing process from within. However, it has no time frame of recovery, and honestly it is something that will stick with me for the rest of my life. I'll never be able to forget it. But I had to move on with my life and not let it consume me. He just didn't want to hear that.

"I'm going to get that fool he said!

Watch, and I can't wait." The look on his face, and the darkness in his eyes assured me that he was going to do exactly that.

"He said this fool had the nerve to report to my First Shirt. He told him he was afraid of me and he felt threatened due to the circumstances, so I can't be nowhere near him when we at work.

"But if it's the last thing I do Storm, I'm going to get him." He yelled. It ant like he can hide. The dumb fool live next door and I work with him. I see him at home and at work.

"I'm going to get him!" He vented.

"I'm going to get him!" He repeatedly yelled.

Lately, I've been having the same nightmare, I told Carter about it as it seemed so surreal. Ever since that night I haven't been able to shake it, for some reason that nightmare kept coming back every time I attempted to get some sleep. So, I've been sleep deprived trying to escape that dream.

"He asked what kind of dreams keeping you up like that?"

I keep dreaming about you and a baby. Like you knocked some bitch up.

"Storm!" He said with a surprised look on his face. "You ant got nothing to worry about baby. Unless you're pregnant already. I'm planting my seed in you tonight. I've been trying to get you pregnant for many years now." His voice sounded like never before and he said it with such conviction to make me a believer in what he said. "You're going to give me my son he said with a southern twang!" He told me, then grabbed my ankles sliding me over to his side of the bed. The rest of the night was sparks flying, emotions going, and passionate love being made.

The next morning when he left for work I started snooping around his apartment sure to find something. I went and looked in the closets and I saw a couple guns. There were three up in the top shelf and a big riffle leaning amongst the wall in the corner of the closet. I then went to the kitchen and looked in cabinets only to find pictures of unknown females. One in which it looked like he took on a road trip. The scenery suggested to me that he visited his mother with some chick.

I found a big yellow envelope on top of the refrigerator and couldn't believe the official documents that I read. It stated that Carter was both bipolar and schizophrenic. The documents also explained that he had to take medication and needed to undergo continuous psychiatric treatment. I couldn't believe what I just read. I kept starring at the documents in shock more so, in disbelief. While sitting on his bed I couldn't help but notice the stack of journals along the wall. It seemed as if there were hundreds of them. I looked over at the clock and grabbed up a few of them. I still had a little time before I had to be on the yard for my first class. I couldn't help myself so, I continued to do more snooping around. Why did I do that? I was always told that if you really do not want to know the truth than don't go searching for the answers. I can't say I didn't want to know the truth but was I ready for it?

All his personal thoughts were thoroughly and carefully documented, and described but at this point exposed. It was as if he was crying for help by telling his story. I found out that he recently had two girls pregnant at the same time, one in which were expecting twins.

They lived across the street from one another so he was having problems with the both of them competing for his time. I read that they were both in the military and he took them both shopping to Baby's- R- Us for the baby's needs. Then one of the females lost the baby, and got out of the military.

He further explained that the medication that they had him on was not helping him at all, in fact he felt as it was making him worse off mentally. The more I read the more light was shed on what he had been doing, going through, and his inner thoughts. I continued to read and turn through the pages barely able to see as tears where just flowing nonstop. My stomach had turned in knots with emotion. The reality was that everything that hadn't made since made since now. I was holding the answers to all of the BS he put me through. This was the reason why he was suffering with mental illness! Being that we've been out of touch recently. Who would have ever thought he had enough time for all of this to transpire. I was in Shock to say the least as I didn't see any of this coming. He did a hell of a job hiding all this from me, it was if he was living multiple lives, who was this man?

I couldn't read anymore I grabbed a couple of his
journals, locked up the house and left. I wasn't in any
condition to go anywhere so I called off work and just
didn't go to class. My heart felt as if it was ripped out of
my chest and walked all over. He really did have a baby
on the way, and my night mares were premonitions of the
near future. Once I got home, I couldn't help but keep
reading the journals over and over, and each time it felt
like a knife was stabbing me in my heart. I couldn't
believe all the things I read. My jaw dropped, and I didn't
know where to begin when I called mommy. It was all too
much. Can you imagine planning to spend the rest of
your life with someone only to find out that it was un-
authentic? Or was it?

The thought of what I just recently read made me
want to get tested again. Not only for pregnancy but for
all STD because obviously he had been doing the most
out here in these streets. Here we go again, I thought to
myself as I had a flash back of James and his deadly
secrets. I took the pregnancy test and anxiously waited on
the results. That three minutes that the instructions
recommended seemed like the longest time of my life.

It seemed as if the clock stopped as I had a feeling this was a pivotal moment in life despite all the shenanigans. If it was negative, I vowed to leave for good and never look back. And if it was positive I would need them to test the baby for mental illness while still in the womb.

I couldn't believe what it read. So, I went to the store and purchased three more just to double check.

"What in the hell was this?" I thought to myself. In disbelief, this test has to be wrong. I yelled.

After I took four pregnancy test I drove over to Miami Valley, the local hospital's emergency room. Yes this was an emergency! The nurse came in the room and asked me what brought me in today? I told her that I took multiple faulty pregnancy test and that I needed her to draw my blood to confirm the results. She looked at me with confusion and asked me to be clearer. I further explained that I'd been bleeding for over a month. I've also been feeling drained, ill, and weak with no energy so I decided to take a pregnancy test.

"Ma'am if what you are saying is true, first we need to take a pregnancy test to make sure that you are not having a miscarriage and if you are in fact pregnant.

I need you to give us a sample of your urine so we can make sure everything checks out.

After a few minutes she came back in the room. Yes, it is confirmed just like you said, the pregnancy test was positive.

The doctor shortly came in after and said they were sending me upstairs to get an ultrasound to figure out exactly what's going on internally.

"From there we will do a DNC if we need to because it looks like from all the bleeding, you may be having a miscarriage."

I looked at him as if he were speaking another language. I didn't have a clue as to what DNC meant.

"Excuse, me what does DNC mean?" He must have seen the look of confusion on my face because at that point he immediately began breaking it down in simpler terms for me to understand I'd never heard this term. At that point I looked over at my mom, I just laid there nervous, dazed, speechless, motionless, and confused yet again. For some reason a strong since of grief came over me. I began to cry as reality sat in. My emotions were all over the place. This news was just devastating.

I needed reassurance because this was all too much to swallow. I had to call Carter to tell him what was going on before I let them do anything. As soon as he answered the other line I blurted out,

"Babe, I'm in the hospital and you need to get here as soon as you can."

"What's wrong?" he frantically asked?

"I'm pregnant!" I yelled as I burst in tears sobbing like no other.

"Why the fuck are you crying? He yelled.

"What's wrong you should be happy that's what we wanted, right?" He said anxiously.   I paused a few moments trying to gather myself as I was crying profusely.

I heard a female voice in the background. The first time I thought it was me tripping so, I ignored it only to hear the voice again. It was a female she asked Carter, "Who was he on the phone with." Ok, so whoever it was wanted me to know that she was there now it's two thirty in the dam morning. What was she doing at his house I thought to myself? I had to play it cool as I could not focus on that right now.

"Who is that?" I asked.

" Oh, that's Monique He responded nonchalantly. "I'm over here helping her get packed up. "She's moving to Florida and she taking my son with her.

"Son? What the hell are you talking about Carter?" I yelled.

"What son?" I screamed!

"What are you talking about?" I frantically shouted.

I instantly thought back to when he first came back from deployment.

"Remember when you didn't tell me you was back, and I drove to Kentucky and you didn't answer the door. She was there wasn't she?" It was her. It was then I screamed. I figured it out.

This happened then didn't it?" I yelled.

We need to talk he said cutting me off in mid-sentence.

"Which hospital are you in?" He asked.

I was in total shock! I felt like I was about to pass out from hearing this devastating news, as I didn't know how to take it. Hell if I did I was in the right place for it.

My heart started racing, I started sweating

profusely, and the walls felt as if they were closing in on me.

"I'm at the same hospital I always come to, ant nothing changed around here but you! " I said in a smart, cynical nasty tone!

"I'm on my way." He told me as if he didn't just drop a bomb on me.

All I could think of was; who did he get pregnant and was my dream really a premonition? My mind was racing nonstop.

"What's wrong baby?" My mom asked me after seeing the look on my face and hearing parts of the conversation. She walked over to my bed. "What did he say, what the hell is going on Storm?" I really didn't feel like explaining so I just laid there silently in my hospital bed. Even though my mom didn't know exactly what happened, she knew something was wrong. She held me tight and told me that whatever was bothering me, put it in God's hands and everything was going to be alright. Baby, Mommy is here.

All I could think about was all the years I'd given this

man. I even tried to bless him with a children of our own for years, but hell his ass already had one. I was pissed! He was living a double life and I was flabbergasted to say the least. What about all the doctors' visits to see if fertility was possible? Was the foundation of our relationship all a lie? Why was he so adamant about starting a family with me if his intentions lied elsewhere? I went through all this shenanigans with this man only for him to knock some other women up! Why did he lie to me when I told him I dreamed about him having a baby? I was in a state of shock, just couldn't believe it!

Due to female complications, the doctors told us for years that we more than likely won't be able to have children. So, all I could think about was how was I pregnant now? This was more so a bitter sweet moment. Especially since this news came short of him telling me he has a newborn baby. I thought I was in twilight zone, if there ever was one.

After entering the room for the ultra sound, the tech told me to get undressed from the waist down and that she'll be back shortly. I was physically shaking, my mind drew a blank as I didn't know what to think.

I was just nervous and on edge. But pissed off at the same got damn time. I laid down and started crying more just thinking about it all.

She poured the cold gel on my stomach and pulled out this big object that was a replica of a penis.

"Insert this inside of you. She Instructed me. It's a camera." She said.

 I looked at it and inserted it in me. She then asked "Do you hear the heartbeat?"

"The heartbeat!" I repeated in shock. "The doctor just said that I was having a miscarriage. She said well if you are then you must be carrying multiples because it looks like you are about four months and two weeks pregnant today. Look right here she said as she pointed on the screen at the sac and live baby.

Moments later she wheeled me back down stairs where my mother was still patiently waiting. "What did they say? "She asked.

I started to explain to her what happened during the ultra sound and the doctor walked in. He said ma'am after the ultra sound and blood test. It looks like you are confirmed pregnant and currently high risk.

At this point we are concerned. You were pregnant with twins and it looks like you are passing one as we speak. So you need to lie down, stay off of your feet, and take it easy. Let's just wait this out for now too see what happens with the other baby. In the mean time I need you to follow up with your OBGYN, immediately for further observation."

I was still shocked, trying to take all of this news in. Now I have to find a way to explain to him that we were pregnant with multiples but we lost one. To God be the glory, the other was still alive.

Carter walked in when the doctor was almost done talking so he was able to hear the tail end of the story and directly from the doctor's mouth. The focus went off of my doctor as Carter entered the room at that point. I wanted to punch him with all my might, but I just didn't have the strength in me.

I just cried, screamed, and cursed at him. I honestly didn't want him there at this point. But I had no choice in the matter. Within a days' time I found out that I'm in my second trimester of pregnancy, may be having a miscarriage, and Carter has another baby.

Hell I was emotionally drained at this point. I didn't know how much more of this I could take. This was truly exhausting and a roller coaster ride of a day I thought! My eyes have obviously been wide shut as I didn't see any of this coming.

"I can't believe I went from having no kids to two kids. This is crazy! "He said excitingly to happy.

I was so upset I didn't know how to respond. In fact I was afraid to because I didn't know how I was going to react. This was heart wrenching, and devastating news. I cried all night just thinking about it.

The next day I drove over to his house with his journals in hand. The ones I took the other night. When I pulled up I didn't see his truck so I grabbed my stuff, snatched some tape from the glove department and headed towards his apartment. I started looking around to see if anyone was outside, or looking out the windows but there wasn't a soul around. The coast was clear. No one was outside and it looked like the mail had just ran and he hadn't checked his mailbox in days. So I decided to stuff his journals in the mail box and taped the ultrasound on the screen door for everyone to see.

I looked around again and seen no one was looking so I was clear to go! Whoever that chick was on the phone last night I wanted her to know that I too was pregnant because I know he didn't tell her. This was the only thing I thought to do as I hadn't a clue who she was. So all I could do is catch him off guard, and hopefully she would be with him. All I can say is Love will make you do, say, and act certain ways. A few hours later my phone rang. It was Carter he told me that we needed to talk!

Being pregnant was not comfortable, I was sick all the time but I did not allow that to stop me. I had to find a way to keep on pushing on at all cost. I had to continue working and going to school fulltime as usual. I was determined not to let my health stop me. On top of that, I had to make time to go to the doctor a couple days a week to get check-ups as well. Getting up was starting to be more difficult, and the doctors wanted to put me on bed rest because I had a high risk pregnancy considering the circumstances. I couldn't wait to have our miracle baby and hold him in my hands!

So, all these visits was enough and drama going on in my life with Carter was not the focus of my life, not right now. All I wanted was positive energy and no stress if you ask me. In this moment it was not about us it was all about our unborn son. At this point I was soon to have our blessing, a beautiful baby boy. And I wanted to keep him inside of my stomach for as long as possible. The doctors said the longer the better chance for survival. My pregnancy was rough but Carter was by my side to make it easier as best he could. He took me to every doctor appointment with the exception of three, and that was because those where unplanned visits. I have to say when he went with me to the doctor He made me feel comfortable as he asked more questions than I did. He was very knowledgeable about it all. He'd filled my prescriptions if they gave me any, and would make sure I ate. He'd also take me to work, school and pick me up every day. I couldn't ask for a better partner to bare child with. I have to admit he spoiled me rotten. Being that he worked in health care he simply had that nurturing spirit and you could tell because he had a warm hearted grace with it all and was very natural at taking care of me.

I want to say everything was peachy with us in the relationship department even though we did not live together everything had been going good for us lately. But I was starting to get a feeling that there was another women. These red flags were consistent and kept popping up because he started getting messy in my eyes. The last few nights he picked me up from work and brought me back to stay at his place I couldn't help but feel some type of way let's call it a women intuition to go searching. He shared an apartment with a roommate. Here lately, I would find stuff here and there.

One particular night when I went over there he had his son that was two months old at the time. When I walked in his roommate Iman was sitting in the living room with his fiancé playing video games and drinking beer. When I went into his bedroom Carter was giving his son a bath. He looked like he was tired, warn out and stressed, the baby was crying so I took over without hesitation.

"Let me do it" I said, as I grabbed the wash cloth from his hand and started washing his face.

He said, "I got it."

"No, I'll do it Carter, just go." I calmly said.

He told me that he was going to go warm us up a plate then kissed me on my forehead ever so gently. Ok, I said as I continued to bathe the baby and attend to his needs. It was my first time meeting him at this point he was now two months old. I was washing his tiny handsome self- imagining and practicing as if he was my own. I had my own baby due here in a few months and it was my first child. I couldn't help but stare at him as he looked just like Carter. I wondered if this is what our baby would look like, or was he going to look more like me? I couldn't help but think. Giving jr., a bath inspired me and gave me hope of something to look forward to as this would soon be my reality in the near future. Although, I was still messed up mentally that he had a baby by another woman and he had a baby that was older than ours after all this time we had been together on and off..

It was like we hadn't been together and trying all these years. Deep down inside I was hurt but couldn't wear it on my shoulder. I was still in shock, and numb about this fact. But every time I look into this tiny little baby boys eyes all that went away. I'm too spiritually blessed to be vindictive! I loved this little boy already!

After I gave him a bath he was fast asleep. I then wobbled in the living room to see Carter had ate his food and meanwhile started playing video games. I guess he forgot about my plate. I went back in the room because my sneaky behind seen that I had ample time to snoop. I peeped back out into the hallway and looked down only to see Carter tossing back beers with no intent on coming back in the room no time soon. So I looked in the closet and didn't see any female clothes. I looked high and low. After not finding anything I headed towards his dresser drawers and didn't see anything out the norm, however, I looked on top of the dresser and seen a note book paper with names on it. It appeared they were on teams as it read Carter and Nisha versus Iman and Kim. This little information gave me a lot to go on, as it told me they were coupled up. And my question was; when was she here? I'd been over here every night this week. Wow, I wanted to look no more. This was enough! If I kept on my search there was no telling what else I would find.

When he came back in the room I was lying in bed with the baby watching TV. I was upset and pissed off to the highest of pistivity.

"Are you ready for your plate babe?" He asked.

I ignored him. He repeated, "Storm are you ready for your plate."

"I'm not hungry" I replied.

"What, do you mean you're not hungry? He asked seeming confused.

You're pregnant, and always hungry. What's wrong now Storm?" He asked.

I just gave him the evil eye and asked "Who is Nisha?" I asked with a serious face.

He stood there looking at me in deep thought, like a deer caught in headlights wondering where I got a name from and who I had been talking to. I just started laughing as I instantly grew angry, and irritated pregnant and all!

He said "she is just a friend."

"Do I know her?" I asked him with the side evil eye.

"No. But what's the big deal Storm?" He answered already in defense mode.

"I see this chick was here while I was at work. My main question is why she can't come over while I'm here."

Oh, babe there you go tripping again for no dam reason. He said.

I picked you up from work to let you relax. You didn't even do that. You're pregnant and you don't need to go getting worked up like this for nothing" He stated.

Calm down "You have my baby boy inside of you. He told me while rubbing my belly. He then signaled for me to come lay on him.

You know I don't want anybody but you! We are going to make this work baby I love you! Hearing him and seeing his action was two totally different things. All I knew is that I was soon to have our baby. Being high risk and all. I was determined to have my baby no matter what so I was going to have to start taking it easy and try not to let life get to me to much despite all of what Carter put me through.

The pregnant life was starting to take a toll on me lately. Even though I was high risk, and the doctor wanted me to keep my unborn child in for as long as possible. Being confined to bed rest I couldn't take it anymore. My feet were swollen, I could barely walk, and I was in and out of the hospital a few days a week. I grew tired and miserable. All I wanted to do was give birth and get it over with. I was anxious to hold my son, and see the life that we created. I went to the store and purchased two bottles of castor oil then rushed back home, packed up our hospital bags and sat at the kitchen table starring at the bottles. I was contemplating because I knew more than likely this would make me go into labor. But, was I really ready?

After drinking both bottles I impatiently waited to see what happened. It seem like it took forever because I fail asleep waiting. Three hours later I woke up in excruciating pain. I felt my baby dropping , I started to hear noises from internally then the contractions started coming and not going. I went into mommy room to wake her up. Mommy its time, it's time I yelled!

I immediately called Carter, and told him that we were headed to the hospital. He grew excited and asked

"Is it really going to happen this time babe?"

Yes, I screamed. I drank castor oil. You did what he yelled in a high pitched tone? You better pray don't nothing happen to my son because of no stupid stuff.

"Why did you do that Storm?" He yelled.

I hung up the phone, because I was not about to be doing this not right now I was in labor and all I cared about was getting to the hospital and safely delivering my baby. Upon arriving to the hospital Carter had managed to beat us there. He came to open the door and carried me in to the maternity room doors. While my mother went to park the car.

They checked to see if I had dilated, at that point I was at five centimeters. But the baby heart rate kept dropping. They said I had to undergo an emergency caesarian. I instantly grew nervous as the look on the nurse face spoke volumes I knew it was not good.

"I told your stupid ass you shouldn't have drunk that shit!" Carter yelled.

The nurse looked at the both of us confused.

"She said what did she drink sir?"

She drunk castor oil, and I told her she shouldn't have done that he said with a southern twang.

The nurse face turned beat red.

"She said why would you do such a thing?" I looked at her rolled my eyes and started screaming "Ouch, Ouch, Ouch", I had another contraction, and the last thing I wanted to do was continue to discuss anything with this women or anybody else for that matter.

In minutes they were prepping me for surgery. They said one person at a time so my mother and Carter traded off. She couldn't stomach the smell of burnt flesh so she decided to wait outside the door for Carter to give her an update.

"Are you okay baby, he asked in excitement."

You are about to have my baby boy. I was so happy I started to cry just thinking about it. He wiped my tears as they rolled down my face. All I felt was pressure from them pulling, cutting, and grabbing him from under my ribs. The whole time Carter kept looking at me and back over the curtain. It killed him that he couldn't help deliver his own son. I was joyful that this moment was really here and I was actually about to be someone's mother, this was a blessing.

Holding Armando for the first time was very special, I had to literally fight with Carter to get my mommy time in. We noticed that his breathing was irregular and alerted the staff. They rushed in only to have him immediately transported to a more specialized hospital for children after discovering it was a respiratory issue being he was premature. Carter stayed with the baby, and I stayed behind at the hospital as they restricted me to leave considering I just had a Cesarean. I felt lost, all I wanted to do was be with my baby.

Now that the baby was born things have changed. Having him changed my whole outlook on life and how I viewed it. It was almost like our son, filled the void that I never knew I had. He gave my life meaning, and I felt blessed to finally have him home and healthy.

A month after Armando, was born Carter came over to finish up the baby room. I wouldn't know a hammer from a nail. Me and tools just don't work well together. When I looked over at the window, I couldn't help but notice his truck parked outside still running, with the lights on. Babe, "I yelled why you leave the car on?" Because my girl in the car! He yelled.

"Your girl!" I repeated in confusion.
 Everything stopped. What. Since, when did you get a girl friend? Why didn't I get a memo? How in the hell do you have a girlfriend when I just had your baby? We just had sex last week so when did this happen? I was lost, confused, and speechless.
"Life with you is so unpredictable." Carter. You've taken me on a roller coaster ride of emotions for the last time!" I feel like I'm jumping through hoops and running through fire for you Carter, and for what? You don't appreciate me and I'm tired of it!

After what he said really resonated with me moments later I said

"Okay so you just reckless out here you get me and another women pregnant at the same time, and now you have a new girlfriend.

"What are you doing? I yelled.

"How dare you put my life in danger like that?"

You got me all the way fucked up! I yelled out of frustration. I got a lot going on right now, way too much on my plate Carter. Maybe I should just step away and gather myself, I need to focus on me and my baby and work on Storm. You've been doing too much out here lately and there is only so much I'm going to take. I'm not cut out for all this drama Carter. Remember that, I don't need a man I want one. I don't need you I wanted you. But all this extra stuff you've been putting me through is too much. I love you but I love myself more Carter.

You don't give a fuck about us! I screamed just leave. Just leave I cried. I startled the baby because he started to cry. Carter tried to attend to the baby but I yelled just go! You've done enough you shouldn't keep your girl in the car waiting! I said with attitude as if I cared.

The reality of us not having any other choice but to co-parent and not actually be together quickly became quite evident. However, that pill was a little hard to swallow. Even after everything that we'd been through. It almost felt like we were bonded beyond the physical because for some reason we just couldn't stay away from each other. One thing is for certain, no matter where I go, or how much distance between us he'd never let me mentally get too far. But I was determined to finish school regardless of all of this I returned to school three days after having him and graduated the next in a month in a half later. I had to find my inner strength to deal with all of this, not to mention walk around campus after major surgery with staples still in the stomach, and drive to class everyday for five classes. All I can say is "Thank you God!"

MENTAL WARD

Not to long after returning back to work after maternity leave. I had just clocked in at work when I heard my phone ringing. I rambled around my purse or should I say my duffle bag looking for my phone while rushing to sit down at my desk. When I saw it was Carter coming across my caller ID. I was shocked but immediately, answered because I hadn't talk to him since the big blow out.

"Babe what's up?" He said in a faint voice not sounding like his usual self or more like he just woke up.

"Nothing much. Just at work what's going on?

"I'm sick and I need you to bring me some food." He faintly told me.

"What's wrong? Where are you?"

"I'm in the hospital." He said.

"The Hospital! What's wrong? What hospital are you in?" I asked.

"I'm in the V.A in the psych ward."

"What do you mean you are in the Psych Ward?" What the hell are you doing there? How long have you been in that place, and why?" I didn't let him answer as I was too busy asking more questions.

"Calm down babe I had an episode. We will talk about it when you get here."

"No. We are going to talk about it now, I yelled! What the hell is wrong with you and why are you there?"

"Man, babe, I started hearing shit."

"Hearing what?" I so rudely interrupted.

"I been hearing shit like voices, and I can't sleep. Ever since I came back from Iraq I can't get this shit out of my head. But I don't want to talk on the phone so I'll talk to you when you get here." He shortly clarified.

"Oh, and Storm, can you bring me some Chipotle?" He asked me as if he didn't just tell me that he was hearing voices.

"So let me make sure I heard you right you want me to sneak food in the mental hospital?" I asked him. "I know that's not allowed so, what exactly do you want me to do?"

"Yes what you think!"

"Ok, well I'm on my way" I hung up the phone. I clocked out and headed for the door in a frantic rush. I jumped in the car and called my boss to call off. I ended up telling her that I had a family emergency. After getting his food I headed to the V.A. Driving around that place was confusing to say the least because they had buildings for everything it seemed like. All I seen was buildings and graves for miles and miles it felt like. They had different streets that lead to nowhere like a big maze. Not to mention it was raining and you have to drive twenty miles per hour with the address being little numbers on tiny little signs. I couldn't see anything, hell I didn't even have my contacts in! After what felt like eternity I found the mental ward. I had to sign in and state my relation, and the time of my visit. I looked at the log and flipped through pages because I wanted to see if anyone else had been to see him. It was no telling how long he had even been in this place or whom come to visit. Nothing looked familiar at first glance so I kept looking in hopes of finding something like inspector gadget. I looked at the log and back at the lady behind the counter as I was sure to be caught. After a last glimpse of the next page I seen he had three unknown female visitors, and his good friend Iman within the last two days.

When I opened the door I couldn't help but notice him grinning from ear to ear. I'd never seen him look so terrible! A tear started running down my cheek before he could get to me. I had never seen him like this and we lived together for years. His hair was nappy, face unshaved, pale, and he looked as if he hadn't showered or ate in days. He had on a hospital gown, with the matching blue pants. He worked in the hospital so the last sight I was custom to seeing was him being the patient, and a mental one at that. This was not him nor was I willing to accept this as him because he was better than this!

The closest that I have ever been to a mental ward was seeing it on television. I felt like a little kid on a field trip exploring life and looking at everything. I saw a tiny little window with bars to protect someone from breaking the glass. There was also a bed and the room was all padded.

"Why the hell are you in a padded room, Carter? What's this about?" He giggled, and started to walk towards me grabbing his food out of my purse placing the bag on the bed beside him as if he was starving. Then he turned my way palmed my ass and passionately kissed me on my lips, then my neck. Let's just say he was wanting a lot more than just food.

"What the hell are you doing? Carter stop! I pushed him away. "Why are you in this place?" He started kissing me more passionately, while at the same time ignoring my question! "Please answer me!" He backed me against the wall pulling my dress up and my panties down. He said I missed you baby! "Boy if you don't stop I said jokingly. I'm not going to lie, he was turning me on. "This cannot go down like this.

What are you doing? Someone is probably watching us."

"They don't have cameras in here." He replied still fondling me.

"How do you know that, this is mental ward for Christ sake and a secure area at that?"

"Do you see any?" He asked me.

"Well, Carter what if someone comes in? You are in the dam mental ward, so expect the unexpected we are not at home, with your crazy ass!"

"Dam, I said jokingly is that all you think about? The whole time while refusing he was proceeding to touch me in all the right places, and my loud screaming no don't do that stop, became silent whispers of don't stop, Baby please! All I could do is stare at the door the whole time and pray that no one walked in. How embarrassing would that be? It felt as if I was more focused on the door then being in that intimate moment. Because the last thing I wanted was to be caught in this act. He could care less who was watching, and someone catching us was the last thing on his mind. He was acting like a squirrel trying to get a nut as if he hadn't had none.

He had his mind made up, and I ran with it as usual. Carter just had a way of talking me into doing things I knew I shouldn't be doing. I would have never thought this morning when I woke up that today's agenda consisted of calling off work and going to visit Carter in a dam mental ward. I don't even think having sex in a mental ward even made my bucket list, nor my agenda for the day. But I guess I can add that and check it off at the same dam time and looking forward to it.

I pulled my panties up, and fixed my dress, checked my mirror to make sure my hair wasn't out of tack, and my makeup was still fresh. We then sat on the bed, watched the rain and ate our food. I looked back over at him and he was still sweating, it was dripping down his face. He started eating his burrito as if he hadn't ate in days. I started to feel sorry for him as he looked like he had been dealt a bad hand lately. All I could do was wonder what was going on. Something obviously had been going on and I don't know what exactly but something wasn't right with him.

"Babe I needed this. Thank you so much! Ever since I been here I haven't had an appetite." He suddenly stopped eating and started crying.

"I can't get this shit out of my head. I haven't told you everything that I've been going through." He broke down in tears, hugged me tight and put his head against my face and just cried. I just let him get it all out while rubbing him slowly on his shoulder attempting to console him.

"This shit is getting worse." He said. I hear voices, and nothing is going right in my life. Nothing, he yelled. Everything I touch crumble, and I mean everything. I can't take this shit! You are even fucking driving me nuts!" He said.

"Excuse me?" I said confused. At that point his twin came out. And when I say his twin I meant the other personality. By now I was used to it, but I wasn't..

Oh, here we go again! Carter. There is no need for this I said instantly growing agitated. Everything has been just fine, but there you go going off the deep end messing things up for no reason.

"They got me on these meds and it's making me crazy, I've been hearing demons!" He yelled.

"Ok, wait what do you mean when you say you hear demons?"

He cut me off before I could repeat it, "You heard me! I can't get this shit out of my head. I'm not sleeping, I can't eat, and I don't like being around people half the time. I just don't know what to do" He said sadly. I just need help babe!

Well that's why you're here. Hopefully they can get to the bottom of this. You're in the hospital babe so you're in the right place. Just don't get defeated this will probably be a process and not fixed overnight. At least were making progress right? You're too strong for that champ! He smiled gave me a kiss, and watched me walk towards the door. I turned around, just before leaving and blew him a kiss. Call me later if you need me babe, and let me know what's going on. I will he said looking sad to see me go.

GAME CHANGER

Months later a lot had changed. Carter got deployed oversees again. It seemed like every time he went overseas I would always get a weird gut feeling and couldn't stop wondering about what if? What if something was to happen to him, what would I do? Regardless of our status the love I had for this man was undeniable. It was very irritating waiting for the mail or the phone to ring. It suddenly appeared that I was always on edge, and on pins and needles. I missed him so much. I loved him but I had to do it from a distance. He had a new girlfriend, now.

It was her job to do the worrying but I had his son, and I still cared about, loved him so I too was concerned. It was very difficult, and challenging making my decision. But for my mental sake and to stay sane because I'd just graduated from college I decided to relocate to Maryland for a fresh start in life just me and my son. The decision wasn't hard because the last thing I wanted to do was end up in jail for whopping his girl. She has intentionally doing things to my son because she despised me. For example like take him to daycare in the dead of winter without a coat. I really didn't want my baby to be anywhere near her. The last thing I wanted to do was see him, or see him with another women. Putting that aside it was all about the wellbeing of our son. I knew he wouldn't let nothing happen to him, but what about if he wants around. I didn't trust the bitch as far as I could see her after a few intentional incidents. I felt like I had to get away and focus on just me and my son. I needed to turn a leaf and start a new life there was nothing keeping me here. But it seemed like everything was trying to hold me back. Despite all of my motivation and ambition I just couldn't stop thinking about Carter and everything that we'd gone through.

Soon after the move to Maryland I decided to go out and see the city since Armando was in Ohio with his family. I heard DC was chocolate city so I wanted to go see for myself too bad I didn't have my girls with me. Oh well I thought I had to remind myself that this was a fresh start. With no destination in mind, I decided to go in the first bar I seen, but was unsuccessful as it was thirty five and up. Well I wasn't old enough for that one, so I went in a place called Zanzibar, and then another bar directly across the street. I have to say I hadn't seen so many Rolls Royce's in my life. I counted three in a matter of minutes. It took for me to come here to see it as I've hadn't seen not one in Ohio my entire life.

When I entered the place, I couldn't help but notice all the cuties, there were a lot of distinguished looking handsome men. Overall it seemed like a mature atmosphere, and a nice setting until I looked up and saw a half-naked chick dancing on the bar and a few others in the corners in cage looking stages. What in world. I'd never seen anything like it I thought to myself. Once I made it over to the bar, I looked up and seen a tall dark,

African guy. He caught my glimpse at first sight then he came my direction next thing I know he came and sat next to me at the bar.

"Can I buy you a drink?" He asked trying to yell over the music.

Well you sure can, I yelled in a flirty voice.

My name is Chimo, "What's your name? He asked while grinning"

Storm. I replied.

Well Storm he said as if he didn't believe me,

"Are you from around here?" He asked.

No, I said just visiting.

We sat at the bar for at least three hours laughing, talking, and getting to know each other. All I know is he kept the drinks coming but I couldn't help but notice that I was the only one drinking. So, Chimo, That is your name right?

Yes, he said in a deep voice.

"Do you drink?

No, I don't drink, I have never taken a drink before in my life. Well this will be my last cocktail I abruptly said.

"Why is that he asked?"

Because you are not about to get me drunk and take advantage of me.

"I wouldn't do such a thing sweet heart. I just want you to enjoy yourself".

He seemed genuine with his words, and generous in the spending department. He said take down my number and give me a call sometimes, let's hangs out.

Ok I replied, my night went according to plan I thought to myself. I got out the house and met someone and he seemed decent. I can't even lie I got a little excited. Maybe this move was a good thing after all. Chimo was very warm, loving with his six foot tall, chocolate handsome self.

I wasn't looking for a relationship but this brother seemed to defiantly be a good catch. After a few phone conversations I grew more comfortable with him. He invited me to dinner, a movie and then back to his place. After a few long chats I learned that this brother had it all the way together. Chimo had his Masters degree from a top Ivy League school, he owned a three hundred thousand dollar home in DC, and no kids. He was the first guy to interest me since Carter and I split. So you know he had to be special. Things were going well and progressing quit fast between us. So, I decided to tell Carter that I met someone. Let's just say that conversation didn't go over well. I really didn't know what to expect as this was foreign territory. This was the first time, since I met carter that I had moved on, Carter had been my world all these years but now I was moving on. I have to admit it felt weird.

About six months into our relationship I allowed Chimo to finally meet Armando. He kept asking if he could meet him as all I did was talk about him so he felt like he knew Armando already. It was Christmas day, Chimo called and said that he was on his way. What he didn't mention is that he was playing Santa Claus because when he came through the door he came bearing gifts, including a red bike with the horn. Armando, seen those gifts and his eyes instantly grew big. He forgot all about the gifts that mommy and daddy got him.

I have to admit I too was caught off guard. Being in a new state, and hours away from my family during the holidays this meant the world to me and I was so thrilled

to see them hit it off so well. Because only the lord knows
how nervous ,scared and anxious I was as he had never
met or seen me with anyone other than his father. I didn't
play with that.

A few days later Chimo, called and he didn't sound like
his usual happy self.

He said "his mother fail ill, and he would have to go back
home to Nigeria for a while to attend to her needs. He
said his job is allowing him to go remote, so he didn't
know how long he would be away. Storm, I love you he
said and hung up. Days turned into weeks, and then
months before I heard from him again. One day out of the
blue Chimo called me from a number that I didn't know.
It showed extra digits I guess referencing a country code.
Not knowing that strange number, I hesitated to answer.

"Hello,"

Storm? The voice said from the other end.

Yes, I replied.

"It's Chimo, how are you and the boy doing?" He asked.

We are doing fine. I said. Thanks for asking.

"How are you and your mother?"

Well, that's what I called to talk to you about storm he said. Then there was a silent pause. He said my mother has turned for the worse, and I don't know how long I'm going to be here. I don't want to drag you through this with me so I'm sorry storm but we have to break things off between us for now. It's only fair to you he said you're a good girl, beautiful, and smart. I care about you a lot Storm, I really do but we've been moving way to fast and I have too much on my plate right now. I have to go baby girl, bye for now. I'll call you when I get back to America he said as he hung up the phone.

I tried holding back. As soon as the he hung up I burst in tears, sobbing like no other. I didn't know whether to be sad, upset, or angry. My emotions were everywhere. The one decent guy I met ups and leave the country and calls to break up with me. This was way too much I was in dire need of a cocktail or two.

Three weeks later Chimo called from his cell phone, He said he wanted to check up since he hadn't heard from me. When he said that I instantly thought to myself how could I call this fool in Africa? It's not like he gave me the phone number to his parent house. He said,

"I've been working nonstop for the last six months I need
a vacation."

"Vacation, I repeated. Ok, I'm just a little confused
Chimo. Didn't you just get back from Africa?"
There was a dead silence, as if he had to think about it.
"He said Storm, I'm sorry but I made it all up." My
mother is not ill, and I did not travel out of the country. I
lied to you storm. I just didn't know how to tell you that
we were moving too fast."
I was devastated, shocked, and really didn't know how
to respond. The last thing I expected was this and you
think you know people This scared me because you may
think someone is one way but get to know them a little
better and still don't know them .The thought of this was
scary and I knew the dating scene was not for me. Not
right now I just needed to focus on me and my baby. I
was cool!
Carter had been in Kuwait for almost six months and they
were eight hours ahead of us. Being that they were a day
ahead his early morning, and late night calls always woke
me up out of my sleep before time to go to work.

Thank goodness this wouldn't last too much longer because he was due back to the states soon! I finally decided to tell Carter about what Chimo did, but I was reluctant because I knew he was going to have something smart to say more so like and I told you so moment. I just knew it. After I told him what happened.

He said "I don't know why you wasted your time with that fraud dude anyway. "And giggled.

Whatever, Carter I said. He's not a fraud, and you're the one that went and got a teeny bopper. Hell she could be your daughter with her barely legal ass. But whatever, that's what you wanted so that's what you got. I said. Don't throw shade at me and expect not to have it thrown back at you. Ok!

"Storm, he said I didn't call to talk about this babe."

He said I've gotten sick a few times and had stopped eating because the meat was awful. He went on to say that he thinks it was camel meat that they were feeding them. So my whole family sent care packages so that he could eat on various snacks, and get his nutrients he favored to hold him over at least. We sent so much stuff he called and asked me and mommy to stop because he couldn't bring it home and wasn't going to have a chance to eat it all.

"Storm, I sent you something he told me during one of our conversations over the phone.

"Oh, babe you didn't have to go through all that trouble I said. You're so awesome, I love you!"

Deep down I was excited to see what he had sent because he was known for showering me with gifts and sending me goodies from overseas or bringing it back for me. He knew how much I loved collecting unique things especially since he traveled out the country ever so often.

"I sent you a mink comforter and it should beat me to the states."

"What do you mean it should beat you to the states?" I asked are you coming home." I screamed with excitement while jumping up and down!

"Yes, Babe I'm coming straight to you." I have not seen him in months because of his deployment.

"Are you serious I screamed?" I was so excited.

171

"Yes, I'm coming to see you and my son! I'm flying out of Kuwait to lay over for a few days in St. Louis then I'll be landing at BWI, the Baltimore Washington International Airport. I need you to pick me up from there."

"No problem Boo Just let me know what time and we will be there!"

I was so excited I took off work for two days which went into the weekend so I could spend quality time with him, and no interruptions. All I could think about was him visiting and finally coming back from overseas and straight to me just like that. Furthermore, we had some last minute planning and finalizations for our son's birthday party being that it was two weeks away. Mr. Super dad wanted to pay and plan it all by himself really. I sort of had to take a step back even though I was a take charge type of women. I had to let him do it. Armando and I couldn't sleep all night anticipating daddy's return tomorrow. All he kept asking every five minutes is it four o'clock yet mommy? We headed to the airport, about two hours early just to beat the Maryland, DC, Virginia traffic. When we got there I thought I was on base because there were a few hundred men and women in uniform. Some were being deployed out and others were returning back home. There were military and civilians everywhere standing alongside the doors and looking for their loved ones. People were crying, and others shared excitement to see their loved ones return home. While some others were standing around impatiently holding signs, and not wanting to see their beloved go. The moment was pivotal and life changing for many and we stood there witnessing it. It was breath taking to me as I stood there and soaked in the moment. I looked in the eyes of many of them and heard silent screams, cries of joy for their safe return home, and arrival. This was all too familiar.

All I kept thinking was where is Carter? It seemed like we were standing there for an hour or so and the little one started to grow restless.

"Mommy, when is my daddy coming?"

I kept looking at the gate to make sure we were in the right spot and then back at my watch to make sure we were on time.

"Mommy, where is my daddy?" Armando asked.

"He's coming baby, we just have to be patient." I replied. There were military men and women in uniform from various branches all at once. Watching them in passing felt like a patriotic moment. In that moment I had a flash back from September 11. I kept seeing planes go through the building. It was sad knowing all these troops were coming and going on deployment and leaving their families behind. Seeing all the soldiers in uniforms, made me reflect back on the base for a moment. After what felt like eternity he finally came walking towards us. I noticed his walk before anything with his bowlegged ass, then his pearly white smile. He was carrying a book bag, few big duffle bags, gas mask, readiness gear, and a big gun case with his gun inside. He dropped it all to the ground and ran to us. Armando, seen him and yanked away from me! Daddy, daddy he yelled! He had the biggest Kool-Aid smile ever. This was a surreal moment! He then headed towards me and picked us both up at the same time. Giving us the biggest bear hug ever! It felt like it lasted forever he held us for at least twenty minutes as if we were the only ones in the room. I was so happy that he made it back safely and I couldn't help but admire the muscles that he came back with.

I attempted to help pick up his belongings and instantly stopped as it was too heavy.

Stop babe, he said. What do you think you're doing? Let me pick it up I got it.

"How in the hell did you carry all of this?" I asked as we headed towards the car. Lord knows, it was too much for me. The thought of him having to carry this all the time was mind blowing.

 I forgot where I parked and we went walking on two different levels before I was able to find the car. I was so mad at myself because when I went to pick him up I had a one focus mind and that was getting him. What I didn't prepare for was my little car and his big ass gun. I didn't know he had to carry it himself I don't know what I thought I figured they shipped them over there already. My little Honda wasn't big enough, so I left it for him to deal with. I had no clue how he was going to get that darn thing in there. After two good pushes, and a little use of his muscle he finally got it in. I was amazed, but knew I had to drive safely, especially on the 495 beltway with my son in the back seat. Not to mention my phobia of guns, and not to mention it was rush hour traffic. I found it very difficult to maneuver. Let's just say I was nervous as hell. At first I drove in the HOV, lane flying through traffic as that is what I was used to. The HOV lane is the high occupancy vehicle lane for people who are single riders. It's where they can drive in the further lane while freeing up congestion in regular lanes. But it came at a cost. We finally arrived to my apartment and safely. The thought alone was scary.

After we got to the house he first carried Armando in as he fail asleep in the car after all of that anticipation. We couldn't even get up the stairs and in the door quick enough before he laid him down and started kissing on me in all the right places. One thing lead to another. We ended up in the shower, and making out. When we were done I grabbed my wash cloth and washed him down. I started wiping his chest, stomach, and then down to his legs when he said babe,

"When I get back I'm going to put my Armando name right here."

He pointed at his chest beside his heart. I just shook my head.

No words on earth could convince him otherwise so I didn't even try to debate with him. I didn't have any tattoos nor did I believe in them but to each his own. He already had five or six of them including one of his other son. So the issue was dead before it started there was no discussion to be had.

"Whatever, Carter can't nobody tell you nothing so whatever you want just get it! You already know how I feel about that. So, I'll leave it alone. "

Let's just say he stayed a week in a half. We made some of the greatest memories ever, and spent a lot of quality family time with Armando. This time together was well overdue much needed as all Armando did was ask about his daddy the whole time he was gone. This temporary stay made me think of the possibility of it being permanent, and getting back together. Although it wasn't reality to me for real it sure felt good! Cooking three full course meals, shopping, putting him back to sleep and waking back up to him again was satisfying to me reminded me of where we once where, and on everything I loved that's what I missed. That was my comfort zone. Seeing the look on Armando's face made me content and relaxed. This was a priceless moment and one that I wished to capture in my heart forever. Our baby was thrilled that he was spending time with the both of us and together. What more could a girl ask for, I was one proud momma and felt very joyful and blessed about it. That lasted all but a few minutes as Carter kept telling me that he wanted me to move back to Ohio. He complained of the distance, and said it was too far. He wanted to be closer to me and Armando. He frequently mentioned it nonstop while he was there, and brought it up even after he left Maryland visiting. I can't lie, he planted that seed very firm because I couldn't stop thinking about it. I was starting to contemplate the move hard and entertain the thought. In fact I couldn't stop thinking about it. Especially after he left, I looked around seen my son and the four walls. I instantly felt empty and couldn't help but feel like a part of me walked out with him. I felt like I was missing something. Even though all of what I really needed was right by my side.

Later that night, Carter called to let me know he arrived back in Ohio and safely.

"He said babe, I miss you already."

Oh, how sweet, Carter I said in a sweet voice.

"Let's get a place together and be a family again. I miss you. "

He said in a sincere and cheerful voice. Being in Maryland with yawl made me realize what I've been missing. I want you! I need my family back!" He said with tears in his eyes, he was crying I knew it I heard it in his voice.

"Well how do you expect to do that I asked?" Don't you have a girlfriend?

No, I'm done with her.

"Why?" I asked.

"Because this just ant working out no more! I'm cool he said with frustration in his voice. I knew there was more behind that and that he was hiding something.

"Well I'm going to have to think about it because I really like it here. No., honestly I love it here. I've finally found a place where I can breathe and start over, be my own person, and find my way on my own in a place where no one knows my name. It feels good to get to know myself and cut my phone off and be disconnected from the world. Whenever I want. It felt good to not have to worry about no one stopping by or bothering me. So I don't know if I'm ready to give that up just yet." I told him.

"Babe, please!" He said.

I don't like to be alone. I don't know how much more of this I can take. I need you and my son with me!" Now! I need yawl here with me babe.

I really didn't want to respond at that moment as it felt like he wasn't giving me a choice in the matter. I felt slightly pressured and didn't want to make any decisions at this time as I knew that was all it would be. He knew what to say to push my buttons and get me going. He had that much power over me and my emotions. Honestly, I felt like dropping everything and leaving everything behind but I didn't want to make any rational decisions in the heat of the moment and regret it later. That's the last thing I wanted to do.

"Just give me a little time Carter." I said. Let me think about it.

I have to think about all of this, sleep on it for a little bit and get back with you on my decision. This is a major move, you know and a big decisions to make so I have to think it over. I don't want to just uproot so fast when I've just got settled in. In fact Carter, something of this magnitude should be discussed in person, so how about we talk more about it face to face after the birthday party?" I advised.

"Okay, if that's what you want Storm. Have it your way. We will talk about it when you get ready!" He said in high pitch tone.

I instantly knew he was growing agitated. The last thing I wanted to do was upset him or make him mad. So I instantly changed the conversation. On the way back to the airport I was feeling some type of way. I was already missing him and he wasn't even gone yet. I really love this man regardless of anything there was just something about him.

"Love you too big head." I told him in a serious but playful way.

"You didn't give me enough time to miss you" I responded.

We stayed on the phone for thirteen hours yesterday. We even fell asleep on over the phone because he didn't want to be alone. He told me that for some reason, he had to hear me sleep. I instantly thought to myself that it was a good cover up because he was too far to do a drive by. If I lived in Ohio he would pop up as usual and it would be expected to be honest and if he didn't I'd know something would be wrong. He also wanted to make sure I didn't have my new African male friend over, with his controlling self. I knew what he was doing.

I realized I brought Armando way to many gifts for his party, so I shipped them ahead already wrapped just in case. As soon as I landed in Ohio, I went over to Carter's place. When I entered his house the gifts were the first thing I seen, as well as a lot of others. I looked over and saw his fifty inch plasma on the wall, computer stand in the corner, pool table in the middle of the floor, and exercise equipment in the other corner. The house looked like a true bachelors pad. No doubt! There wasn't a women's touch anywhere so that was a little confirmation that everything was going to be okay.

He clearly still hadn't unpacked from deployment as all I seen amongst the wall was deployment gear, and packages. There were large boxes, and tubes piled up along the wall untouched. I then went to look around the rest of the house and after further inspecting I found only one tooth brush in the rest room. I had asked him where his girlfriend was as he had been clinging to me more lately. He said they had broken up and was going through some problems. He said she wants to go to counseling but he was not going.

"I thought to myself counseling, okay so since when do single couples go to counseling?" I'd never heard about that one well unless that was a psychiatric patient, counseling stuff like that but single couples unless working towards marriage not so much.

BIRTHDAY PARTY FROM HELL

I flew to Ohio for our son's birthday party shortly after Carter left from Maryland. We decided to have it where our friends and family could come celebrate together being that we lived in two different states and we had a lot of people in our circle. He asked me to stay at his house for the week. I was a little skeptical more so hesitant as I could do was wonder what if his ex-girlfriend came over. I didn't want to have to put her in her place nor did I want any drama.

The last thing I wanted to do is come home to Ohio, go to jail ,and catch a case for assault and battery. Hell I am educated and know the dam law. So the last thing I wanted to do was get in some trouble. He assured me that there would be no drama and she was no longer a factor.

"She will not be coming over Storm! We're good babe I told you that everything is cool." She got her own thing going on, her own house, and practically a new man. Trust me, I would never put you or my son in harm's way! I will kill someone over mine, I care too much about my family.

Carter picked me up from the Airport. When I arrived he was standing by the baggage claim waiting on me grinning ear to ear. I didn't have my contacts in so, I didn't notice him until he walked up on me. He came from behind and picked me up hugging me tight and kissed me while I was still in his arms.

"I love you babe, and I missed you." He told me while still hugging and kissing all over me.

I'm just saying. Hell if that was the case we should of went a long time ago. No, actually we should be there now! Counseling! Really. How was that possible? I thought to myself. I needed to be counseled for the last seven years, I thought to myself and I stood there and pondered on it for a few more minutes. But somehow his charm and good talking self-made me able to let it go.

We got behind on time and realized we were running late to the birthday party. Let's just say he took us all the way off schedule and didn't have a care in the world as if we didn't have to beat the guest to the party. Men I swear.

While in the shower he grabbed the cloth to start washing my back when I took it from him and started washing his chest. I didn't have my contacts in but I couldn't help but notice his new tattoo. He had the audacity to tattoo his supposed ex-girlfriend name across his heart in the same place he said he was going to put Armandos name. At first glance I couldn't believe what I was looking at but when I continued to scrub it and it didn't come off I realized that this was real.

"What is this Carter, I yelled." referring to that tattoo on his chest. I was confused, speechless, and pissed to say the least.

"What the hell is this? When did you get this done because this wasn't just here when you came to Maryland?"

The last conversation we had before you left, do you recall talking about you was going back to Ohio and getting Armando's name on your chest I screamed. Really. Why would you get permanent ink on for temporary chick? I don't understand did I miss something. I know she's got something to do with this. I said in a serious but sarcastic tone.

What would make you put her name on your heart and in permanent ink at that? I stood there butt naked soaking wet in disbelief, shock and confused of what the fuck I was looking at. I was hurt, to say the least! This was beyond crazy to me and beyond my most analytical thinking, reasoning, of trying to figure it out and understand.

"I thought I had your heart". I screamed, while smacking him in the head with the wet rag!

"Why was I here wasting my time all these years? I yelled.

"What the fuck am I here for? "I was pissed.

"What have we been working on all this time? You've wasted my time, Armando's time and everybody else's involved and for what?"

"Do you love her?" I screamed.

Do you love her more than you love me I asked him? In a firm but serious tone.

I felt so betrayed. For the life of me I couldn't understand why the man that I love and bared child with went and got another women name on his chest. He looked at me with the most puppy dog look ever.

"When you were in Maryland you said where getting Armando name tatted on you but instead you put that chicks name on you!"

"No baby, I love you and only you." He told me.

"I'm sorry! I never meant to hurt you.

"Then Why, Why, Why!" I yelled! "

Tears were rolling down my eyes. I was still starring at this man's chest. I was not able to figure out what this woman did to win a permanent spot on my man's heart within a couple of months. I been with this man for years. Hell every time I tried to leave he wouldn't let me go far and he kept telling me that he needed me in his life. He said we were going to make this work, be a family, and make me his wife. That's the only reason why I stuck around. I guess this was all game huh?

We had to get to the venue a little earlier then everyone because we had to set up for the thirty kids and parents we were expecting. With family, friends, and his military buddies children we were expecting to come out of a lot of money today. We paid for it we just wanted everyone to enjoy themselves. I managed to get all the tables decorated, and gift table set up when I couldn't help but notice more people began to show. When I say more I mean the uninvited.

I started to get irritated thinking about that tattoo it was eating away at me but I was determined not to let that take my sons moment away from me or him.

189

I started looking at all these folks I didn't invite and instantly caught another attitude. People had brought their other friends, cousins, nieces and nephews. All I kept looking at was money spent. This was taking us way out of the planned budget and was a little ghetto if you ask me. Especially if you know that you didn't have the money to pay for it yourselves, but you bring extra mouths to feed. I immediately went and complained to Carter about what was going on and he took five hundred out of his wallet and placed it in my hand.

"Calm down babe, it's our baby boy's day. Just deal with it for right now." He told me in a calm in a loving way. " Go get more pizza so everyone can eat. I looked back at him; he smiled and nodded for me to go. I guess I'm the frugal one today I thought to myself. Wow! I had just got paid so I already had eighteen hundred in my purse. Money was the least of my worries. I just didn't want to pay for some inconsiderate folks that were not invited and knew they would have a good time, and free food at our expense! Uhh over it I thought to myself while walking over to order more food!

About an hour after the party started, we began to feed everyone. He brought his phone over to me look at a video of our son and his brother riding the bicycles together. In the video Carter was attempting to teach the boys how to ride. When that video went off I decided to scroll to the next one, and why did I do that! It was his girlfriend standing up at the stove cooking when I heard him say

"Look at my WIFE'S fat ass!"

Did he just call her his wife? I dropped the phone he looked over at me and frowned. I couldn't believe what I'd just heard. I picked up the phone and gave it back to him. I had to run to the rest room and try to make it as fast as I could because tears started to come down, and I couldn't stop them. I did not want to ruin my son's birthday party but I couldn't help but feel some type of way. More like hurt, pissed, mad, heartbroken, betrayed, and numb at the same time. I started to question if he had lied about everything all this time.

"When did he get married?" I thought to myself.

"Why didn't he tell me?"

"Why was he still sleeping with me?"

"Where had she been all this time?"

All these questions were going through my head nonstop.

Married! It was crazy how I even found out that he was married. Because the one person he didn't tell was me. Did everyone know, or was this a secret?

This brother even had the nerve to" ask me could I help him get a divorce?"

"Can I do what? I yelled."

I don't know how to get a divorce you never married me. You just strung me along, and had me here on false promises and lies. Don't you see that? At this point I was beyond myself and didn't know what my next moves were.

He nervously said "I'm sorry Storm I fucked up." I mean what the fuck is funny?" He had a stupid smirk on his face.

"You told me we were getting married a long time ago. That is the only reason that I've stuck around this long. So, to find out that's not even an option at this point you have cut me deep! All I wanted was to be your wife I cried. All this time you assured me that we were working on our relationship and you up and marry someone else. How dare you?" I yelled.

"I should have lied to you but I told you everything!" I should have cheated on you because you don't appreciate me! How dare you do this to me Carter?" I yelled.

"Why did you string me along if you had no intentions on marrying me?"

I would have left a long time ago but no I've given you my all. And you took my kindness for a weakness! I should have done you wrong but I don't have it in me to do it. I don't I can't believe I've been sleeping with a married man. And who would have knew after almost eight years of being with you!" That I would end up the other women. I was so angry. "There is never a dual moment fucking with you!" I yelled!

"Baby, I'm sorry. Please forgive me for not telling you sooner he cried. I just didn't know how to say it." He pissed me off even more with his apology.

"I swear Carter, I've never been to jail, but the way you keep messing with my head you are going to make me snap!" I told him. "Don't you think I should have one of the first people to find out you were even getting married. I'm the women that you laid down and bared child with you!

"Don't you think I need to meet the women who is around my son"

I need to know if these women are capable of taking care of him right! I told him.

"Let me get out of here before I hurt you!"

I was scared to go back out to the party as I had no control over my emotions. I didn't know what to say or how I was going to respond and I hate when I get like that. I ran to the bathroom to hide because tears started to fall down my face. I didn't want anyone to see me cry my pride wouldn't let that happen.

"Baby, please come out this bathroom. Carter said in a soft concerned voice on the other side of the bathroom door.

"Is everything okay?" He asked.

Let's just get through our son's birthday party and we can sit down and talk about this later. I love you baby and I never meant to hurt you!

I couldn't believe this fool had the audacity to ask me am I ok after I found out about his secret marriage. That really upset me even more. However, for the sake of my son's party I pulled it together and forced a smile on my face. I returned to the party as if nothing happened.

"Is everyone ready to have fun?" I yelled. I was trying my best to put the attention back on my son before I act the fool up in this play land. I couldn't wait for this party to be over, so I could get back to his house and get some answers. My nerves were shot , I somehow managed!

Once we got back to his house we could not get into the door good enough before my questions came flowing one after another. I was truly hurt this time as I didn't see this coming at all. How could he take this from me? He couldn't answer questions quick enough before I started on the next one. I really wanted to know why but I was so shocked, and caught off guard I was hysterical.

In my wildest dreams I wouldn't think of him ever deceiving me this way. I was feeling some type of way or should I say feeling that one way! My emotions were beyond out of control and so was I.

"I love you babe, and I need you! I want to marry you as soon as I get this monkey off my back!" He said, referring to his wife.

"I miss the hell out of you and I'm not going to let you go again! I want to be with you for the rest of my life. I fucked up Storm, and I know it this time." He said "Just let me fix it. Please, baby, I need you in my life." I just want to be a family for my son!

"You did me so wrong Carter and I did nothing to deserve this disrespect." I told him while pulling away from his embrace.

"I know that I've done you wrong and I am regretting that. If I could take it all back I would but I can't. It's just that I thought that you moved on and started a life with that African dude. That was one of the main reasons why I strayed. I didn't know what to do for real!" He gently pulled me back to his arms.

"Let's just work it out baby I really fucked up this time let me make it up to you."

"I just want to make it right, Storm."

"I love you! He said."

He claimed that she told him if she couldn't have him no one could!

"Babe I need you to help me with the paperwork so that I can file for a divorce." He bravely asked me.

"Help me get a divorce babe so I can make this right with you. I want to marry you like I should have done in the first place."

A few days later when I got back to Maryland the first thing I did was research on how to get a divorce. The part that made me feel uncomfortable and weird was the fact that I had never been married. I felt if I hadn't wasted time waiting on him that would have never happened. News flash to me! This just didn't seem right! But he asked me for my help and assistance I was used to helping him with all his personal important paperwork. Not only that but I really wanted his last name, I wasn't his ride or die for nothing. Those where the plans we made and I knew he would keep his promise to me.

After what seemed like days of research I sent him the divorce papers and instructions to file for the state of Ohio. I couldn't help but to let him know that I felt degraded as a women for helping him do this.

"You didn't tell me you were getting married, or after the fact married, so why in the hell should I help you get a divorce?"

He said the only thing he wanted was his name back.

They weren't married for long before they were talking divorce so it seemed like it would be easy to do. They were doomed from the start. Hell she was a kid herself. I still don't know what the hell you were thinking in the first place but that's neither here nor there. You did this shit to yourself.

I didn't know where to start, as I had never been married. So, why the hell would I know how to get a divorce I thought to myself? I looked to google and other resources and searched for a few hours. Once I gathered all the necessary information I forwarded it to him along with all the laws of Ohio, including the proper paperwork to file. He called me right back and said that I was amazing and he couldn't do this without me. I told him to look to the internet for a resource if he needed further help because I was done. Furthermore what he had going on was known of my business. He told me that he loved me, and said that he couldn't wait to see me again. He also told me that he had a beautiful time with me the last couple of days.

"Baby, it just felt so right! It was confirmation that I need my family together, period!"

A few weeks after I gave him the paper work he told me that she had been served. He told me that every court date, there after she was a no show, and refusing to give him a divorce. Talking with him lately it seemed as though he was depressed and withdrawn from a lot of things that he loved and cared about. Life was really starting to affect him. He wasn't eating, as he said he didn't have an appetite, couldn't sleep, heard demonic voices all the time, and was having issues with his Zoloft. I asked him if he had talked to the doctor and he told me yes. All they did was lower and upped his dosage of medicine. He didn't want to continue taking any more of the medicine because he actually felt better when he didn't take it. There were plenty of nights he would call me late to stay on the phone with him so he could hear me sleep because he didn't want to be alone.

He started calling me every day all day. Even while I was at work. I knew something, was wrong. I couldn't get any work done because he kept interrupting me by calling so darn much. However, I had him on my mind just as much as he had me on his, so I was cool with that. He was begging me for help this time like no other. All he kept saying is that he didn't want to be left alone, he didn't trust himself, and he wanted me to move back to Ohio, so we could get a place together and be a family again. This is all I want. He said.

"I fucked up Storm. He told me "Just give me a chance. Please baby, help me get out of this situation and I promise I'll marry you like I should have done a long time ago. Just bring my son back to Ohio." He begged. Let me make it right!

"What about my career and everything that I've established here?" Carter. I can't just give that up.

"Just do it!" He demanded and hung up! I sat there for at least twenty minutes in silence thinking about if I did go back to Ohio to be with Carter would it work or will it fail like the last few times we tried? Was he serious, we're we really going to get married this time, and was I really ready to move back to Ohio? These were the questions that I needed answered before I took that leap back to my home town that I just left. I didn't know the answers but I knew God would have to lead me in the direction because it was in His hands now. I thought back to the main reason I left Dayton and it was him. So, why should I run back now I asked myself?

"Mommy called and said that she was in the hospital and on her way back for emergency surgery."

"What wrong mom? I asked frantically."

"She said I went to my doctor's appointment and they found the arteries in my heart are bad they are at ninety eight percent blockage so they transported me over here to the hospital they need to perform a quadruple bypass today baby."

"What's that I asked?" In a high pitched concerned tone.

She said they will have to take the artery from my legs and place them in my heart baby. So, are they going to take your heart out of your chest? I don't know baby she said. But I'm on my way back to surgery now. I started crying. She said I just wanted to let you know babe.

Ok, mom I'm on my way I'll be on the next flight out of here I said crying. I tried not to cry on the phone because I wanted to be strong and didn't want to scare mommy. But I just couldn't hold back, because I had just lost my grandfather and couldn't stop thinking about him. Lord knows I couldn't handle something like this right now. I was scared, nervous and afraid. How was it just yesterday she was her normal self-laughing, working and today she was being rushed in for emergency surgery in fear of a heart attack? Life was coming at me way to fast. I couldn't stand there and contemplate I had to make some moves and fast.

Wow, what was next I thought to myself? All I could do was call the airport book a flight and jump on the next thing smoking out of here. I could not think straight all I knew is that moms was sick and I needed to get to Ohio and fast. I got to the airport in an hour and took a fifty minute flight straight to Dayton International. I already had a ride waiting for me at the airport. I didn't have any time to waist. All I needed to do was get to the hospital to see mommy. When we arrived I ran past the flower shop only to run in and grab her some flowers right quick. Mom, loves flowers so I thought they would brighten her spirit. The first person I saw in the waiting room was Sony and I hadn't talk to him, since he kicked me out of mom's house years back. He was the last person I wanted to see, and now was not the time for any drama if he wanted to bring it. He just sat there starring me down. Carter had finally arrived with Armando.

When we were finally able to go in the room to see her prep we went two at a time. Sony and I went first. The nurse stopped me at the door and said I couldn't bring the flowers in. My first reaction, was to ask for my money back because she was the only reason I made the purchase. But I decided not to go there. Now wasn't the time so instead of putting up a fuss I through the flowers away. I couldn't do anything but pace the floors for hours, until I eventually dozed off in the chair. Seven hours later the doctor came out and said that surgery went well, she will be in recovery and from there she will be in intensive care for close observation. I rushed back to the recovery room to check on her, when I walked in she was trying to take the IV's and tubes out of her nose, and mouth at the same time.

"Mommy No." I yelled.

"You can't do that nurse, nurse help I shouted. They came running from everywhere. I didn't know what to do and I was too afraid to touch her as there where wires, tubes everywhere.

Being the oldest child, my nerves were shot. The more time we waited the more family came to the hospital. The waiting room was filled to capacity. My nerves were beyond shot and I was past due for a cocktail. But I didn't want to leave momma, I couldn't until I knew she was good. Because her health is not in the best shape right now, I may have to consider moving back I mentioned to my brothers. They looked to me for answers, so I wanted to at least put some options out on the table to know what may be happening in the near future. All I could do was think about was should I stay in Maryland or should I come back home. Regardless of which decision I made it was going to be hard. Right now with all of what's going on between mommy health and Carter this was a lot to take on at once. I had to make a decision, pray about it, and put it in god's hands.

A week later Mom was well enough to go home, but she was not the person that she was before surgery. Now she had to take it easy. She had to were an oxygen mask now, and sleep sitting up in a chair. Mommy was in a lot of pain. Her chest cavity had been broken so moving around just a little caused pain and discomfort. Seeing her like this was unsettling but to know that she is alive was good enough for me. Two weeks had come and gone before I knew it I had to head back to Maryland. I was still confused and not any closer to a decision. But I had to decide. Mommy was my first priority right now.

As the oldest child and only girl, I had to make sure she was good.

The next day I went to my Job sat at my desk and just thought about my life and where I wanted to be. My wants and needs were clashing right now. Was I going to stay here or move back to Ohio? Carter really put the pressure on me lately and going home for two weeks he was still in my ear. It was time that I put things in perspective. I looked up at my supervisor, I knew he was about to come and ask me to run the morning meeting. I looked at the clock and then back at him. I had figured it out. At that point it had dawned on me. I was tired of being away from him, and my family. I wanted nothing but to be back with him for the sake of our family like he said. He seemed sincere this time like he had changed now. He'd been constantly asking me to move, as he wanted to keep us together as a family unit.

Those words resonated with me. I looked over at my boss door one last time before taking a deep breath, pausing and then decided to go knocking on his door. I heard him on a phone conference with the CEO but I didn't care this was urgent and couldn't wait. When I went to the door he took his feet off his desk and took the phone off of speaker and told his boss to hold on just a second.

"Well can I help you Storm." He asked with confusion in his face.

"Sir, I want to say thank you for everything I want to let you know I have some family issues going on back in Ohio, that need my immediate attention and I will need to resign effective immediately. "

I then started to walk away. He followed me all the way out to my car asking me "was there anything that he could do and if I just needed to take some time off instead?"

Unfortunately, I resign.

"Have you thought about this?" He asked agitatedly.

After all of what's been going on, I made a rational decision and quit my job without notice. Ever since I made that hothead decision things have been a little strained around here lately.

I stuck around a little longer because I contemplated leaving right away. I didn't even tell Carter that I quit my job and thinking about taking him up on his offer. The struggle was real. I didn't reach out to Chimo because I hadn't talk to him since he lied, and I didn't want to concern or worry Carter because right about now he has issues of his own. Bills were coming in faster than money. One day, Armando and I were coming in from the grocery store and there was a sign on the door giving three days' notice to evict.

"What's that mommy"? He asked.

I quickly snatched it off the door hoping the neighbors didn't see it.

"Oh, it's nothing, baby I responded it's nothing.

The next day Armando woke me up.

"Mommy, mommy, what's for breakfast"?

He asked while he shook me awake.

"What I asked dazed and confused, still in a deep sleep."

He was sitting over my head in the bed.

"What is it baby? What do you want?" I asked.

"I'm hungry mommy." He said impatiently.

"Ok, give me a minute I said as I rolled out of bed.

I went to cut the light switch on in the kitchen and it was
still dark. I flicked it again. The same thing happen.
I instantly started to cry. I knew BGE had disconnected
me.

"Mommy, mommy, why are you sad Armando asked.
I just stood there staring at him. I reached as he jumped
up in my arms.

"Mommy, why are you sad? What's wrong?"
I'm not sad baby I replied I'm happy I have you in my
life. Everything is going to be okay I assure you baby. You
are my motivation I said! I just stood there, in deep
thought motionless. I had been praying for god to show
me a sign about moving back to Ohio, or sticking it out
here. Carter had been asking for us to come back home so
I didn't make it any better. He said he wanted to be a
family again and for us to come and move in with him so,
I guess a decision had been made for us. I needed help.
I grabbed my son and went to Uhaul to get a one way
rental. I guess god answered my prayers because we were
headed back home to Ohio.   I had my mind made up. It
seemed like for the first time in a long Carter and I were
on the same page and it felt good.

I was in the U-Haul truck on my way back to Ohio
when Carter called and told me he changed his mind
about moving back in together. As bad as I wanted to
curse him I kept my cool and remained a lady. So, I
decided to hang up on him.

No good would come of me showing up with our
stuff, but he chose a heck of a time to tell me he has re
considered. I was mad, upset and hurt just thinking about
the reasoning behind his sudden change of heart. But I
could not dwell on that or be mad at no one but myself
because he got me once again. I just called mommy and
told her there was a last minute change of plan and I
would be staying with her for a few days until I find a
place for us.

Shortly after I moved back to Ohio, and settled in.
Carter phone calls were far, few and in between. He had
done a complete 180. Day by day he seem more distant.
He always seemed bothered, or like he had something on
his mind. The daily phone calls turned into once a week,
the popping up daily became once every couple of weeks.
I didn't know what was going on with him.

I just knew something was up and whatever it was I was sure to find out in due time. I thought. She must have been back at his house and trying to work on their marriage. I didn't want to pry, so I did all of what I could to keep busy. I picked up more hours at work, threw myself in to my studies and even started going to the gym. I kept myself productive and positive. Armando, on the other hand, was sad and confused. He did not understand why his dad wasn't calling nor popping up to the house like usual. He went as far as running around the house calling his dad name looking in every room. That was confirmation that he really missed him.

Armando and his dad were inseparable so, this drama or whatever it was Carter had going on was beginning to affect my baby. When the phone rang or if there was a knock at the door Armando hoped it would be his father. Carter started to be to no avail these last few weeks and this was unlike him so I knew something was wrong.

Out of the blue Carter called.

"Storm I need to talk to you!" Carter said on the other end of the phone. I told him that I was asleep and that I would call him in the morning. Hell I was tired.

"In the morning, Girl, I'm outside of your door baby, so open up!" He said impatiently.

"Outside!" I repeated.

"Boy, why didn't you call me first, you need to stop popping up cause one day I'm not going to let you in. It's three o'clock in the morning.

"Are you serious?" I asked him.

"Yes, I'm serious so open the dam door girl. Its cold out here he said "before he hung up the phone. I went to the door and there he stood drunk as if he barely made it over here. This is really starting to get old. You show up when you want, it doesn't matter what time it is! He just looked at me.

"Where's my boy I want my boy" He said.

He's sleep you need to be quiet before you wake him. He went straight to Armando's room and jumped in the bed with him. I took my behind back to sleep.

The next morning somehow, he and Armando ended up in my bed with me. How in the world did this happen I thought. As soon as I woke up they got up to. Armando was so happy to wake up to his daddy. Da Da he yelled. He said you got some breakfast food babe? Yes, it's some bacon, eggs, and other stuff down there. He said okay ill cook for us. I looked at him in shock. I was still waiting to find out what's been going on. He said come on Armando, let's go cook mommy breakfast. They left out the room, and I rolled back over until I heard the smoke alarm go off. Let's just say I ended up being the one cooking breakfast.

Over breakfast we all sat at the table, and I said grace. It was silence in the room until Armando yelled Amen. Carter said babe I don't know what's wrong with me but I think I need some help. I'm hearing shit, I can't sleep, and I think I'm going crazy. I keep telling you Carter, you can't deal with this alone. You will drive yourself crazy and the rest of us.

He said "I keep trying to get help but nothing is working. I'm tired Storm, I'm tired." We sat at the table for about an hour I just listen to him talk, and vent about everything.

For a few days he started calling way more than usual, thinking I was in company by another man for some reason. I knew that I needed to leave him alone, but it seemed impossible with all of his pop-ups and frequent calls. He was refusing to let me go, even though we both knew that he did me wrong. He was not going to continue with me, his wife, and all these other women. I refused to allow that.

A few months had passed and everything had changed, drastically in the blink of an eye. It seemed like Carter was going through something again because he started to become absent. Only this time it even felt different. I know we were not on the best terms lately but it's never stopped him from calling every day and coming to pick up Armando. It seemed like he just didn't care about anything anymore because he use to pride himself about boys, truck, and living life to the fullest. I couldn't help but notice all those things seemed like they weren't important to him anymore.

It felt as if he was withdrawing from life and everything he loved. I don't know, maybe I am being over emotional, but one thing is for certain he has changed. My woman's intuition kicked in and is telling me that I'm right and something is really wrong. I instantly grew concerned and afraid.

THE NITE THAT NEVER ENDED

2009 was the year our lives forever changed. This moment in time was pivotal, and the point of no return. Life as we knew it would be no more. This is the day that I never saw coming, my eyes were wide shut. My faith, patience, and life was tested. I couldn't believe they cut his dam phone off. I was pacing back and forth on the sidewalk in front of Carter's apt. complex. I felt tired, helpless, afraid, panicked, and concerned for Carter and his life.

All I could do was sit and wait helplessly, hoping, praying for a miracle. His friend Terrance spotted me and came over to the car.

"Storm, I can't believe this shit! This is unreal". He said.

It looked as if he had been crying.

"Carter just left my house around four so he could get ready for work." Terrance explained

"Next thing I know, I look up to see police surrounding his apartment during the breaking news. Life is crazy man!"

I could not hold back my tears. I was crying and shaking hysterically. I grew more frustrated and agitated by the second, I felt helpless. I couldn't think of anything to do to help him out of this situation. I started to feel like I was going crazy because I was so concerned.

"Baby girl, Stop crying."

"Everything is going to be alright." Terrance said trying to console me and calm me down as we stood there helplessly in the cold.

"No, it's not, you can't say that."

"They cut his phone and power off! Do you not see what's going on here?" I screamed.

All I want is for him to walk out and not be carried out. I just wanted to go in and get him! The last thing I wanted was him to feel alone, and backed against the wall. I could only imagine how he was feeling. That's all I kept thinking about.

I felt like I was about to go crazy at that moment. I didn't know what to do or where to direct my anger and that was scary. All I knew is something had to be done, and fast. I grew more and more frustrated by the second. When I looked over at his apartment building I saw a robot looking machine. I couldn't help but wonder what was going on inside his apartment. My mind went racing. "Storm, Storm!" Terrance yelled, Did you see that?"

"See what?" I asked looking around, thinking he was talking about Carter. "No, I don't see him." I irritably shouted.

As I was looking towards his apartment something caught my eye. "What is that robot doing moving towards his window?" He asked.

"I don't know what that is, Terrance. I yelled as I instantly grew more agitated and anxious.

Moments later the negotiator came back over to us. He said the subject is expired. I looked at him with all my being, and asked what does that mean? It felt like everything around me paused. I didn't take my next breath until he responded.

"He's deceased ma'am.

I instantly grew weak. It felt like the world stopped.

"Why? "I screamed

"Why? "

"What happed I yelled."

He shot himself ma'am." He coldly told me with no emotion.

I lost it, I think I blacked out because I threw myself at the negotiator. "Kill me, Kill me!" Mautha fucka I yelled while launching and reaching for his gun. He stepped back.

"Ma'am, you don't want to do that." He said in a serious tone.

Our son was closely watching me feeding off my energy, crying and holding on to my leg for what seemed like dear life. I fail to my knees please tell me sir, tell me it isn't so!"

"Just tell me please! Tell me please I screamed!" I didn't want to believe it. I just wanted to wake up from this bad dream. "This could not be real I shouted!"

I held my son, and I held him for dear life, as if my life depended on it! All I could think about in that moment was Armando, and how this was going to affect him in his future? What was we going to do now?

I was mentally checked out, and was beside myself. All I could do is cry, scream, yell and curse again. The only man that I gave myself to was lying dead in there and for what? I was hysterical.

The police officers standing nearby came over and said they were refusing my driving privileges because I was too emotionally distraught. He further explained that I was hysterical, traumatized, and in no condition to get behind the wheel.

"Ma'am, we are concerned for your safety, so we're going to escort you and your son down to the station. You can call someone to pick you up from there."

I did not hear him. All I seen was his mouth moving. I was numb and mentally in a place I'd never been. I stood there in shock and disbelief. Everything just happened so quick it felt like a bad nightmare.

Armando and I was riding in the back of the police car on our way to the Fairborn jail, while Carter was lying dead in the apartment with a bullet in his head. That was all I could think about, my mental and emotional state was. I cried, screamed, kicked and punched the air. I was mad at the world as this just could not be real. "Mommy, Mommy!" Armando cried as he sat next to me.

"I want my daddy?"

Now that broke my heart knowing that his daddy was gone forever.

When we arrived to the jail, the investigator sat us in a conference room.

When I finally looked over I seen a phone sitting on the desk so I reached for it while realizing that my hands were shaking beyond control. I felt like I was having an outer body experience and watching my every move in slow motion.

I called my mother to let her know the bad news but I didn't have the words to explain.

"Hello mom?"

Once I heard her voice I just broke down.

"He's gone, ma! He's dead!" Tears were falling nonstop.

"Mommy why are you sad" Armando asked, while whipping my tears.

"They won't let me drive so I need you to come down to the police station. I told my mother while trying to comfort my son. She broke down, I broke down. We just cried on the phone together.

"Baby, I'm so sorry. You stay put, I'm on my way!" My mom assured me while hanging up the phone.

I couldn't help but stare at Armando, and wonder about his future. He was two years old and now left fatherless in this evil world. What where we going to do now? How was I going to explain to him that his father was dead? He was not going to be there for him growing up, graduating, going through puberty, marriage, needing manly advice, nothing and for what? As soon as I was about to get more emotional an officer came into the room?

"Have you got ahold of anyone yet ma'am?" He asked.

I looked at him but couldn't speak, my mouth wouldn't open, I couldn't answer I was numb. All I could do is repeat what just happened over, and over again in my mind.

The officer returned shortly after. "He said ma'am your mother is here. She's out front waiting, please come with me." He told me I stood up feeling weak at knees and faint. All I heard was

"Ma'am are you okay?"

I tried to catch myself from falling but I collapsed to the floor. When I regained consciousness mom was kneeling down holding my head in her hands, crying and screaming for me to wake up. Officers had surrounded me at this point. When I realized the reality of the situation and that Carter was dead I began crying, screaming uncontrollably again.

My stress levels was through the roof. My phone kept ringing I was in no mood to talk to anyone but it was a Kentucky area code so, I answered. It was Carter's little Brother Derrick.

Derrick kept calling me after I made the call to his mother in Nebraska. I felt she would have never knew had I not called. Carter's wife didn't have the decency to call and inform her or other family. It had been months since Carter's mother and I talked.

I looked at the phone it was Derrick calling again. This was the fourth time so I knew it had to be important. He was the brother that you'd call for backup if need be. Stayed in jail that didn't have any warm smiles, never had nice things to say and didn't speak back when greeted. So I was sort of intimidated to speak with him that night or any night to say the least. But I had to talk to him now!

21-GUN SALUTE....

The day before the funeral, everyone that was in his will arrived at the designated hotel that was chosen. Upon arrival I didn't know how to feel being face to face with the other woman that he had bared child with. Looking at Monique at first glance all I could see was that she was very pretty. Unlike the others she was a step up. She came walking, looking just as broken as I did. Her eyes were puffy, but she, unlike me, managed to comb her hair. She was holding her sons hand. He looked so much like Carter, it was if I was looking at him.

Once she sat down at the round table Armando' half-brother, Junior looked up and saw me. He grinned at me and came running jumping in my arms. I was glad that he remembered me. It felt good after all the diapers that I had changed of his. You could tell that he hadn't the slightest clue of what was going on just like Armando. Junior was just as innocent minded as Armando. I felt for the both of them. Knowing that their life was forever changed. I broke down in tears. Monique looked over at me and held my hand. I squeezed back as we both shared the same grief, and pain. Despite any differences we may have had the fact of the matter is both of our boys were left fatherless.

Later that night after the meeting we all had with the Casualty Military representative to discuss some of Carter final wishes and the next steps of the funeral process. I had a few cocktails. I guess that was the liquid courage that I gathered up. Because I was finally able to sit down and talk to her. It was about time we sat down and introduce ourselves and have a women to women talk. I knew nothing about her besides what he told me and it wasn't much. We were at the point of no return.

It was time to Open Pandora's Box, but was I ready?

Within a four hours span both our emotions went from crying, laughing, getting mad, to crying and laughing again. It seemed we had a lot of similar experiences with him. We found out a lot of what he said was true, but camouflaged more so twisted with lies. In the end we all got played and had to move on from here to make sure the boys were raised right with structure and faith in God, despite the absence of their father.

The next morning we were standing over the casket still in disbelief as the last thing I would have ever imagined is seeing him like this. How does someone go from being a great person, wonderful father, respectable man, go to work every day, perfect credit, never call off work, healthy and physically fit with his whole life ahead of him, to being dead on behalf of his own hand? I just stood there holding my son's hand in disbelief. Armando looked up at me with his small beaded eye with tears rolling down his face.

"Mommy shhh, Da Da sleep!"

I was speechless as the last thing this man was doing was sleep and my son didn't know that he was not going to ever wake up again. He was only two years old standing their looking at his father lying in a casket. I just couldn't believe that the first funeral our son attended was his own fathers. Reality was too hard to grasp or accept. My eyes had been wide shut as I didn't see this coming, nor was I prepared!

I didn't want to acknowledge or accept that this was the way it was going to be from now on, and that he was really gone and forever. The reality that he was not overseas nor was he in training in another state for a temporary period of time was frightening to me. This was way too much and too fast! Carter was actually deceased and never going to be in our physical presence again. Our son was left here on earth without his male tour guide, role model, and confidant of a father. What about when he needs him for guidance, learning how to fight, prom, or when he gets married, graduation, college, first girlfriend, relationship problems, life and whatever is thrown at him I kept thinking to myself while Armando stood their looking up at me.

The thought alone consumed me, it kept flashing in my mind and I couldn't shake it as this was reality.

Armando and I sat down in the front pew in the church. Seeing his casket for the first time sent chills through my body. Shortly after we arrived Carter brother came over and stooped down to me, I grew freighted as he caught me off guard. He scared the hell out of me. He whispered in my ear "where the fuck is she?" I was totally startled and confused with his question.

"Who? I asked him.

"You know who!" He said with a frown on his face.

"The bitch that did this shit to my brother?"

What? I asked in total sincerity, and confusion in my face?

I was shocked to say the lease. My eyes kept starring at the bulge in his pocket as it couldn't have been anything other than a pistol. I knew that he was on one. Hell he was on two! All I could do was think about the possibilities, of what if Carter's wife walked through the doors? Was she bold enough? Hell if she was it would defiantly be another death at the funeral.

I didn't even want to think about it.   Imagine that! I'd had enough.

On the way to the cemetery we were riding in the limousine with all the family: his grandparents, aunts and uncles, cousins. His father and mother drove separately. This moment seemed surreal as I couldn't believe we were going to lay him in his final resting place. I mentally considered it his new permeant address. This was going to be the last time we seen him. I couldn't quit crying just thinking about it. Tears were running down my face like water dripping from a faucet. My phone rang, I ignored it only for it to ring again. I hadn't answered it in days but something told me to get it. I hurriedly scrambled through my bag and finally found it the last ring.   I looked at the screen and couldn't help but notice it read all zeros. I knew this was a hospital but who was it now?" I thought to myself. My nerves were shot, and I knew I couldn't handle anymore".

Hello. Hello Storm, this is dad. What's going on?" He asked me.

"I'm riding in the limo on our way to the grave site".

Out of nowhere he said, "I love you!"

"I love you too dad? Who's in the hospital, and why are you calling me from there?" I asked.

"My wife tried to kill me"!

"What the fuck do you mean?" I screamed.

"She stabbed me an inch away from my heart." He explained.

My heart sunk, almost like the other night when Carter died. I couldn't believe what I was hearing, and I was not in any mindset to handle anything like it. "Not now dad. This is way too much for me to handle right now." I said as I hung the phone up and turned the dam thing off. I didn't want any calls and didn't want to talk to anyone as I felt myself falling further into depression. All I really wanted to do is be away from the outside world.

I was just over my dad house the night of Carter's suicide and my dad's wife was the one consoling me. So why would she do something like this to hurt me even more and try to take him away from me? His wife tried to kill my dad not even five days after my son's father killing himself. This was way too much for me to deal with. I was mentally starting to shut down and all I wanted to do was be alone but out of all times, now was not the time.

We finally arrived to the grave site after what felt like forever. We all started to unload the cars which stretched over a mile long. Everyone that walked from afar all came walking towards the front where we all stood watching the six men and women in uniform marching beside and holding his casket. The United States flag lied smoothly across the casket without a wrinkle. We were all mourning and walked slowly behind it. The music glared from the side speakers. A group of armed men stood to the side with their guns drawn in a motionless salute. There before the casket sat six chairs where the special invites of Carter's sat. No wife to be found I'm just saying. Armando kept kicking my seat "Mom can I get a flower. " He kept asking.

I was saddened after all of the explaining I tried to do he was still not realizing what was really going on.

The pastor said his final words and at that time the military did their full honors twenty one gun salute.

I'd never been to a military full honors funeral so this was the last thing I expected. The sound of the bullets being shot startled me and my son. It pierced me as I kept thinking where did he get the nerve to even pull the trigger on himself? He had too much to lose!

One of his female friends started singing I'm going up a yonder, when a few others let a dozen doves, and few dozen balloons go in the air. It felt like this was all a movie scene because it was so beautiful. When it was all over I was one of the last people to go to the car as I stood there starring at the casket in disbelief of it all. I couldn't pull myself to leave him there by himself. The reality of this gravesite being his new home, did not sit well with me as I never seen this coming. This was the place I would be bringing my son to visit his father from now on. No longer would we be visiting his house, no more pop ups, hugs anything. He was no longer a phone call away, or had our back, or going to be readily available like he'd always assured us. The thought of him not being able to see his kids have children, or show them how to be men, be there to help them through life and its journey made me feel ill. How could he do this?

AFTER MATH

Eight weeks later I finally decided to check the mail. There were piles of it, had I not decided to check it today the mailman probably wouldn't have been able to fit anything else in it. While peeking through it I couldn't help but notice an envelope labeled official business from the V.A., amongst the pile of bills, and junk mail. I hadn't a clue as to what was inside this envelope, so I instantly grew a little anxious. I opened it and quickly tossed the other mail to the side. I began to read the first line when my heart immediately felt like it skipped a beat or two and then a few more. I continued reading when all my emotions and feelings came to the forefront.

In that moment, Eight years of mixed emotions came out and I couldn't stop. It felt like grief and reality smacked me in the face all over again. It was Carter's death certificate, DD-213 forms, and a Casualty Report from the Department of the Air Force listing his two children, me, Monique, his wife and parents. This felt like a blow to my heart all over again it was as if I just got the news for the first time. I couldn't stop crying, sobbing or thinking about Carter being gone forever. The letter attached stated that my son was considered a war orphan. I didn't like or understand the terminology and didn't want to accept this fact. I had no understanding as to how they could deem my baby an orphan when he still had me. This made me start to think about what if. What if something happen to me, which is all I could think about? God forbid that happening as Armando would be left here on this earth without parents? I couldn't imagine that and this reality was a bit much to swallow. Seeing all of this in writing confirmed that he really stood by his word we had nothing to worry about, Carter took care of his responsibilities,

I was grateful but I'd rather have him alive. All I could do was think and wonder what was I to do now?

A lot was changing and fast, quick and in a dam hurry! These last few weeks my life has been turned upside down and Armando's life was forever changed. In the blink of an eye I feel like I've been to hell, redeemed myself, came back, and could possibly be headed back again. My life was all over the place. I didn't know if I was coming or going. All I could do is take it one day at a time. I kept thinking to myself which was a constant reminder that "I'm now literally a single mother with a two year old son to raise alone in this scary, unpredictable world. There was no possible way to contact his father if there was a problem, ailment, graduation, marriage, anything. He was gone forever.

I instantly grew upset when I realized how challenging everything was going to be without him. I wasn't able to call him when Armando gets sick, or have someone care for him other than myself. I was left to groom him into a young man, teach him about life and prepared him for everyday living and whatever life throws his way. I had to teach him how to treat and respect women. How was I going to explain that to a male child that looked up to and admires his father? This was not fare to him or me! Now he was left looking to me for everything. Love, nurturing, guidance, and everything that goes with life growing up, protecting himself, being respectful, and to teach him how to be a man. Now how I was going to do that I had the slightest clue. I just couldn't believe I was left to raise him and try to show him how to be loving, strong, respectable young man all alone. Despite the mental issues that Carter suffered from he was such a wonderful person and I looked up to him in a lot of ways. He showed me the ropes to life, how it was to be strong and maneuver through life with your head held high regardless of what you have going on. He showed me how to be responsible, how to stand up for myself and what I believed in. He gave me our son. Thanks Babe. You left me with a backbone, and the strength to keep it moving! But what I would ask if I could, is how could you show me these things and leave.

Now Carters physical appearance was no more and I was left looking to no one other than the Man above and our son! I had found God for sure then. It was quite apparent. No one left to turn to, and the only man that was there readily available for me to call on was God. But for some reason I ignored all of the signs and the messages he was trying to deliver. All I knew is he was trying to tell me something. I came interdependent on booze. I continued to hear my heart talk but, hearing those words was quite shocking considering it had been years since I last stepped foot in a church. But when you are just about given up on life like I had, in a state of shock, battling depression, grieving and heavily contemplating suicide, who better then God to explain your problems to. No, He didn't physically speak but He put his hand on me and led me in the right direction as I had my mind and heart open, I had nowhere else to turn.

The feeling of hopelessness, lack of energy, the fire of motivation and drive that was once lit was no more it had dimmed. The ambition well had exhausted dry right before my eyes. It was challenging, which is an understatement and very difficult to carry on after Carter's death. I was emotionally drained and depressed.

I could care less about life or anything in it anymore. Nothing mattered and as hard as I tried nothing would up lift me out of this funk. I kept experiencing suicidal thoughts, and didn't see a way out. I got to the point where each day that passed felt like I was going deeper in a dark whole of depression. All I could think about was giving up on life. I had lost close family members, but nothing ever felt like this before. I lacked the motivation, and didn't know where to go from here. Everyday became a struggle within itself, I just had to take it one day at a time.

I turned to the bottle, smoked cigarette after cigarette. Everyone watch as my life began to unfold, and dreams started too unravel. All I looked forward to was smoking, drinking and going back to sleep as I didn't want to deal with reality. I began to lose weight, my hair was falling out, face started sinking in, and acne broke out all over my skin because I wasn't eating, I didn't have an appetite and I wasn't taking proper care of my body properly. I cared less as to how I looked and barely washed my ass. I had begun to give up slowly and withdrawal from life as nothing mattered anymore regardless of how hard I tried. Suicide was all that kept flashing across my brain.

It kept playing in my mind as if it were a commercial. I couldn't get it out of my head.

My mother saw me, and tried to help but I kept shutting her out in fear of letting her close to me. She stressed to me that I was all Armando had left. She grabbed my arms and placed my hands in hers. She said baby don't be selfish and leave him in the world alone. Daddy is gone but Mommy is still here and you need him as much as he needs you. I know what you're going through but I can't say I can relate to how you feel. What I do know is that you and Carter loved each other, and he would want you to carry on and take care of Armando. I think you should seek counseling as no good can come to you self-medicating and grieving the way you are no good will come of it babe. I hate to see you like this!

I started lacking the mental motivation, strength and the want to move forward. Every time I would think about my reality I'd burst into tears. Those two little beaded eyes starred at me with a since of emptiness. Every truck that resembled his father's he would holler out Da Da. Every man in military uniform, or if we pulled up to someone house he would ask was his Da Da in there. It's sad that not only was I going to have to later explain that his father was a veteran of the

Iraq war, and been deployed numerous times but he is deceased and never coming back! Furthermore, he took his own life and committed suicide when he was just a little boy. Those facts alone will drive anyone into despair but the impact that it will have on a young black male is all I could think about. All I could do was hope that the boys wouldn't question themselves when old enough. That was the last thing I wanted and I really didn't want to ask. My biggest fears is that it will plague on his self-worth, self-esteem, and confidence, and that was the last thing Carter and I wanted. I only know this as I grew up in a single family home; my father made bad decisions and was in prison during my prime. Growing up without a father was very difficult and challenging! I could not understand as to why others kid's around me growing up had fathers that were involved in their lives, dropping them off at school, showing affection, being active genuine fathers. I secretly despised it, but I knew one day if I had children I would be married!

Every day it grew to be more difficult, I didn't have the strength to do anything. I didn't want to see people, answer the phone, or talk to anyone. All I wanted to do was get away from it all .

Family, friends everyone with the exception of my son. He is the only reason I continued to live and not give up. My son is my blessing If it wasn't for him I was mentally ready to give up. I kept contemplating suicide myself, battling depression, and stress. But I knew that wasn't an option. I had to change up my environment and get away for a while. I just wanted to get as far away from Ohio as possible. Without notice I packed up three bags of clothes for me and my son and got dropped off at the nearest greyhound bus station with no destination. We ended up getting a one way ticket to nowhere really because I was undecided as to where we were headed and could switch it up the first chance I got. I didn't want to give any one the chance to talk me out of it, tell me I was running, or try to convince me otherwise so I was determined to get way, I didn't tell anyone I was leaving. I didn't want to make contact or communicate with anyone. So, all I could think about was what our my next move? Where was I to go from here?

Jr and Armando took to each other and were really close. It seemed that Monique and I really formed a bond as well. I never thought that this was possible considering we both fail for and was in love with the same man without ever knowing it. In this time it's as if children can bring people together in a special way. Because that's exactly what the boys did. We both loved that man and wanted to keep his two children together and for them to get to know each other. The good thing is they have formed a bond that cannot be broken regardless of how many miles away they were from each other. In the summer when they spend time together its always big brother little brother and competition against each other they are both so much like Carter it's scary. The sad part is when it's time for them to leave one another they always plead to stay together. Their love is bond.

EPILOGUE

TWO YEARS LATER

I was sitting in my back yard watching Armando swim, when my phone rang. It was one of Carters military buddies also known as his partner in crime. He hadn't called in a while but he always checked in on us every so often. He was a breath of fresh air we always talked about the past and went down memory lane together so I looked forward to his calls as he witnessed firsthand what we went through. This time when he called he seemed a little down, and different from his norm. It almost felt like he wasn't looking forward to the call or he had something on his heart. I don't know whatever it was I knew something was wrong.

"Do you have a minute to chat?" He asked.

"Yeah sure, what's up?"

He then asked me if I was sitting down.

"Yeah, sure why you ask?"

"I've been wanting to tell you something for a while now, but I've been hesitant."

Hesitant about what I asked? Confused and clueless as to where the conversation was going at this point?

He said I don't know how to tell you this Storm but Carter was sleeping with another woman before he died. The girl just got in contact with me a couple months back because she just recently heard about Carter's passing. She said she had been trying to get ahold of him but to no avail." He further explained. I was still confused as to what he was trying to tell me and where this conversation was going because at this point I didn't want to hear anymore this was irrelevant I thought to myself.

"Ok, so why are you telling me this?" I asked.

"Well storm, she has his son. The boy looks just like Carter, and he was born after he died. I thought it would be good ideal if the kids know each other since they may be brothers you know. She wants to know if you would allow Armando to give DNA. I hung up the phone quick, fast and in a hurry and refused to hear anymore. This was not the Maury show nor was I about to entertain that. I instantly thought. My chest started beating fast, the room started caving in, and it felt like he just poured salt in an open wound. I couldn't breathe. I started sobbing just thinking about it.

How was I to believe such a thing?

Why was he telling me this now? I thought to myself.

Where did this chick come from? I couldn't stop
thinking if there where any others I heard there was.

Thoughts were coming in my head faster than ever. I
grew frustrated agitated, and pissed off to say the least.

All I wanted to do was pick up the phone but who could
I call, he was dead. I had to call Monique and see if she
knew anything about this one.

THE END

Message from the Author

"Today, I'm still standing strong before you after all of what I've been through. Throughout my journey I learned the hard way how to never put a person living in the flesh before GOD, and self. I'll never hold on to anything tighter than my kids and god. I was able to walk away from these experiences armed with the knowledge of my weaknesses and have turned them into a positive learning experiences to never make the same mistakes again. Each trial, and all tribulations that I've hurdled and walked threw has taught me how to be a strong women regardless of what life threw at me gracefully and with the mask of a smile."

"In order to weather the storm, and defeat the enemy during your trials you must be able to take each day as it comes, and deal with whatever life throws at you systematically but not alone! Be steadfast in thinking, fast in sleeping, prayed up and aware of your actions set before you at all times. In my darkest moments, I was able to find and seek guidance from the man above. He delivered me from all the evil thinking, and the depression that almost swallowed me as well. I love life, and all of what it has to offer. My eyes are wide open now, and I'm able to now see clearly that I still have life's blessings bestowed upon me."

How do we cope, for the sake of life? Well we all grieve and process lost differently however, throughout my pain I had to suppress my feelings so my son could live a fruitful life. I had to take me out of the equation and channel all of what little energy I had in my blessing; my son. He guided me through the light, and gave me the strength to carry on when all I wanted to do was give up. Now surprisingly, I have a beautiful daughter. So, two meaningful, precious lives to continue living for! The way I know how to go about doing it is to stay motivated, Love yourself, Love others, live and cherish every moment!

God has blessed me and delivered me through a lot. My life and experiences has allowed me to grow as the women that I've become and I hope my book can help you in any way. My journey is to bring about attention and shed light on such prevalent issues such as Suicide, PTSD and Mental Illness, Rape, Aids, and Abuse.

ABOUT THE AUTHOR

 Chatiela Underwood is a native of Dayton, Ohio. She is a single mother of two beautiful blessings. Ms. Underwood, attended Trotwood Madison City Schools, and graduated from Paul Lawrence Dunbar class of 2000. She is a college graduate of Central State University class of 2006. She obtained her Bachelor of Art degree in Political Science, and she also studied Criminal Justice. She went on to further her education where she studied at Kaplan University for her Masters in Criminal Justice Executive Management. She later decided that public leadership is where her interest lied and a better fit so She is currently a Master Candidate with Capella University class of 2016 where she is studying for her MPA.

Chatiela is very active and engaged in the community and the education sector. She has passionately worked in higher education and directed schools across the country in business development for over ten years. Ms. Underwood, loves to spend quality time with friends, family and writing, and traveling. She also is a Motivational speaker and truly believes in inspiring others through her testimony. She is sophisticatedly passionate about making a difference in the lives of others, and was encouraged to share her compelling story by writing her debut novel "Eyes Wide Shut."

If you need information on tour dates, bulk books purchases, book signings, speaking engagements for live events, or want to purchase "Eyes Wide Shut" Gear, coffee mugs, Please visit:

ChatielaUnderwood.com

Info@ChatielaUnderwood.com

Follow Chatiela Underwood on

 / AuthorChatielaUnderwood

 @ChatielaU

22 Soldiers Veterans Kill Themselves Every Day.

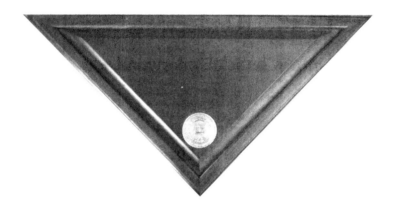

For the first time in the world history more veterans who fought in a particular war have died from suicide after the war than the number of troops who have died in the war .

Mr.Conservative.com

Sotu.Blogs.cnn.com

After reading this story and you know someone whom suffers here are just a few resources:

* We do not endorse any of these organizations.
* Not all listed are crisis.
*These numbers may not be 24 hours.

National Suicide Hotline trained volunteers and professional counselors

1-800-suicide or 1-800-784-2433 available 24 hours.

National Domestic Violence — Rape, Abuse, & Incest Network

1-800-799-3224

For information on free Aids testing

https://www.gettested.cdc.gov/

1-800-232-4636

I hope someone may find this information useful.

ABOUT THE PUBLISHER

31 Woman LLC provides publishing and other services within one company. For more information on books, products and services, visit **31WomanLLC.com** or write to:

31 Woman LLC
7915 S. Emerson Ave Suite B-140
Indianapolis, Indiana 46237
Info@31WomanLLC.com
317-643-0769

Coming Soon to 31 Woman LLC

When The Power Goes Out: Darkness Follows

By Charlotte L. Brown

The traumas that plagued Manuela Richards' childhood followed her into marriage. Despite the circumstances, she fought to hold on to her sanity, husband and salvation until the stress of life plunged her into a whirlwind of hellish events. Will Manuela overcome adversity or will she drown in the belly of death?

Genre: Fiction **ISBN:** 978-0-9835534-4-1 **Price:** 14.95

Available June 2015

Order additional copies of *Eyes Wide Shut*

Chatiela Underwood
7915 S. Emerson Ave. Suite B-140
Indianapolis, Indiana 46237

Please mail_____copies of *Eyes Wide Shut*

_____
NAME

_____
ADDRESS

_____
CITY/STATE/ZIP

_____
PHONE

_____
EMAIL

Quantity	Price Per Book	Total
	15.00	
Sales Tax (OH Residents $1.09 per book)		
Shipping and Handling ($4.99 first book 0.99 each additional book)		
Grand Total* (payable to: Chatiela Underwood)		

*Certified checks and money orders only
Available on Amazon.com 6/1/15

CPSIA information can be obtained at www.ICGtesting.com
Printed in the USA
LVOW06s1117150415

434682LV00001B/1/P